She handed him the letter from England. "Here," she said. "Here's my dad's address in England. If I tell Sharon what you told me, you can write to my dad and tell him . . . tell him . . ."

"Tell him he's completely screwed up your life?" Paul suggested.

Melinda couldn't help laughing. Paul was laughing, too.

"Parents love hearing that," he insisted. "Especially from another continent. What should I tell your mom?"

"Tell her I haven't done one single productive thing since I got here. Not one thing."

"Ah, the do-nothing conspiracy. Guaranteed to make even the best parents question their competency."

Melinda giggled. "Tested by satisfied teens everywhere."

They parted. "Remember to do nothing today!" Paul called.

Melinda called back, "I can do more nothing than you can!"

MARGARET WILLEY is the author of *Finding David Dolores, The Bigger Book of Lydia,* and *Saving Lenny,* all ALA Best Books for Young Adults, as well as *If Not for You.* She lives in Grand Haven, Michigan, with her husband and daughter.

THE
MELINDA
ZONE

❖

MARGARET WILLEY

Margaret Willey
VBYC
1994

LAUREL-LEAF
BOOKS

Published by
Dell Publishing
a division of
Bantam Doubleday Dell Publishing Group, Inc.
1540 Broadway
New York, New York 10036

ISBN: 0-440-21902-7

RL: 6.0

Reprinted by arrangement with Bantam Books for Young Readers

Printed in the United States of America

May 1994

10 9 8 7 6 5 4 3 2 1

RAD

For Chloe

and with thanks to Kate Terry and Bill Baum

How can you love me
if you do not know what hurts me?

ONE

❖

From inside the braking train, Melinda watched her cousin Sharon's figure come into the center of the train window, framed there like a fashion photograph. Something about the way Sharon was waving, with her arm outstretched and her fingers fluttering, something about her perfect blue tube of a dress and her easy, dazzling smile made Melinda's breath catch in her throat. *Sharon is so wonderful,* she thought, waving back. *I'm here. She'll help me.*

A surge of hope came over her, so powerful that it broke through her weariness and so piercing that, as she descended, tears sprang uncontrollably to her eyes. On the platform, she put down her suitcases and covered her face, astounded to be crying. She never cried. Through her tears she saw her cousin's smile fade; Sharon came forward at a half-run and put her arms around Melinda, although Melinda was now considerably taller. Sharon asked softly, "Mindy, what's wrong?"

Melinda shook her head, unable to speak. Sharon

picked up both suitcases and led Melinda to an empty cafeteria at the other side of the station. They sat at a table and Sharon handed Melinda a coarse napkin for her tears. "Did something bad happen on the train?" Sharon asked. She had a new haircut, a tousled cap with jagged bangs that made her green eyes look dramatically huge. She had grown up so much since Melinda's last visit. Melinda felt young and bedraggled by comparison, even in the new clothes her mother had bought her for the trip.

"Why are you looking at me like that?" Sharon asked. "Are you okay? Wait, I'll get you something to drink." She came back to the table with a cup of iced Coke. The fizzy coldness focused Melinda, and she had been very thirsty.

"*Talk* to me!" Sharon insisted. "What happened?"

Melinda found her voice. "I'm so glad to see you."

"Glad to *see* me? Mindy, you aren't exactly acting glad to see me! I don't think I've ever seen you cry before."

"It was hard, being on the train," Melinda admitted softly. "I got upset. And the last few weeks have been . . . awful."

"Were your mom and dad freaked that you were leaving for the whole summer?"

Melinda shrugged uncertainly. "I don't know."

"Which one took you to the train station?"

"My mom. Daddy is already in England."

"Did your mom make a scene?"

"She doesn't do that. I think she was actually kind of relieved. She thought coming here was my idea."

"But it was," Sharon reminded her, puzzled.

Melinda took another sip of Coke, stalling. It wasn't

the right time to explain to Sharon how pressured she had felt to solve the dilemma of where she would be this summer, a dilemma her parents had created with their conflicting plans. "Of course it was my idea," she told Sharon. "But now I'm so exhausted. I couldn't sleep at all last night or the night before and I didn't sleep on the train and I think it finally just all caught up with me."

Sharon pointed out soothingly, "Hey, the main thing is, you did it. You're *here*! We're finally going to spend a summer together—haven't we always wanted to?"

She stood up and gave Melinda's arm a tug, urging her to move. "Come on, I got my dad's car. I told him we might take a quick tour around town. We need a little time to ourselves before you have to start dealing with *my* parents."

She took the heavier suitcase from Melinda and they walked out of the old-fashioned brick station. It was a breezy June night; Lake Michigan was only a few blocks away, glowing to the west from a late sunset. Sharon laughed at how heavy the suitcase was, dragging it into the parking lot. "Hey, girl, do you think you brought enough *clothes*?"

"My mom went a little crazy," Melinda admitted.

"I love that outfit you're wearing. Those leggings make you look so tall."

As if anything could make Melinda not look tall. Sharon unlocked the trunk of the car and hoisted both suitcases in, then held up a set of keys. "Want to drive?"

"I'm fifteen until September," Melinda reminded her.

"Oops, forgot. Your door's unlocked, hop in!"

Melinda climbed in and put her head back, feeling suddenly, unspeakably tired—the tears had taken the last bit of strength from her. The small houses that lined the street to Lion's Park passed in a darkening blur. She squinted sleepily at Sharon, amazed to be with her, really with her, this cousin she had always idolized. Sharon's smile had become more dreamy; her head was tipped, her eyes slightly crinkled. "I want to tell you about this amazing, *amazing* guy I'm seeing now. I can't wait for you to meet him."

"Not tonight," Melinda protested softly.

"Oh, I don't mean tonight, don't worry. He's out of town anyway. But maybe tomorrow night, okay? When I get off work? His name is Evan O'Connor, Mindy, and I am totally in love."

Melinda remembered another name, another boy, from Sharon's Christmas letter. It wasn't Evan; she strained to remember. She wondered aloud, "Wasn't there a Paul?"

Sharon wrinkled her nose. "Oh, him—that was just the guy across the street. This thing with Evan is *serious*." She pulled into a sandy parking lot and stopped the car, facing the lake. Waves were rolling toward them in rhythmic rows, adding to Melinda's sleepiness. "My mom and dad aren't accepting this thing with Evan very well. They think he's too old for me. He's twenty-three."

Melinda's mouth fell open.

Sharon took this as a compliment. "Oh, wait till you see him," she said, giggling. "I'm so crazy about him. My parents will just have to get used to it. But I wanted to warn you. It's making things a little tense."

Melinda confessed softly, "Things have been tense for me, too."

"I could tell from how you sounded on the phone. And it *is* pretty bizarre, both of them making summer plans without talking to each other about it. Even if they are divorced."

Anger swirled inside Melinda's head. "They never talk to each other. They just argue over whose fault everything is."

"Are you mad at them?" Sharon asked curiously.

Melinda looked at her cousin, overwhelmed that she had sensed this much without having to be told. "I am," she said breathlessly.

Sharon smiled a crooked smile, both sympathy and complicity in it. "Parents," she said. "Who needs the hassle? Look at it this way. You are free for the rest of the summer. Totally, totally free."

Free, Melinda thought dazedly.

"And you can distract my parents, so they'll get off *my* case about Evan. We both benefit, see? You've solved everything. You couldn't have picked a better time to come."

Melinda felt tears of relief coming back; she had to quickly look away. It was so much more than she had dared hope for, this sense of purpose about coming. She had been afraid on the train, afraid of her own anger and so unsure of who she would be, this far away from them. She squeezed her eyes shut.

Sharon poked her shoulder gently. "Hey, you, are you going to fall asleep on me right here in the car?"

"I'm sorry," Melinda said, blinking hard. "I'm just so tired."

"We'd better get back. My mom and dad will be waiting to pounce on you. Brace yourself, they are in *ecstasy*. Especially Mom. I had to do some fast talking to keep them from coming to meet you at the train station. I knew you wouldn't want them both falling all over you in public."

"I'm glad they didn't come," Melinda agreed. "Don't tell them I was crying like that."

"Crying like what?" Sharon asked, smiling.

Melinda's aunt and uncle were sitting on their porch swing, Uncle Ted's arm around Aunt Rita's shoulders. They stood up together in their matching gray sweat suits as the car pulled into the driveway. "Come right here and hug me," Aunt Rita exclaimed, coming down the steps with her arms outstretched. There was a koala bear decal on the front of her sweatshirt. She embraced Melinda and kissed her cheek.

Aunt Rita was two years older than Melinda's mother, with a softer, rounder version of her mother's face and frizzy brunet hair where her mother was blond. She was wearing bifocals, peering over the tops of them, her eyes shining. Aunt Rita and Uncle Ted were exactly the same height, both brunet, both freckled and round-cheeked; Melinda had always thought they looked more like brother and sister than husband and wife. Sharon lugged the heavier suitcase from the car and scolded, "Don't attack her, you guys. She's *wasted*."

Uncle Ted took both suitcases, but gasped and slumped over abruptly, as if he'd hurt his back. Aunt Rita was fooled only for a second; then she put her hands around Uncle Ted's neck, pretending to strangle him. He said, in an aside to Melinda, "My wife's a practical choker."

Melinda giggled wearily. Aunt Rita took her hand, led her into the kitchen, eased her into a chair. "Look how tall she is!" Aunt Rita exclaimed to Sharon. "Can you believe it's our Mindy?"

Sharon nodded with a dazzling smile of complete confidence in her own perfect appearance. Melinda remembered something that her mother had said once, describing Sharon: "She's one of those girls who'll never have an awkward stage."

And Melinda had said with a sigh, "Sharon will never have an awkward day."

"It's better to have an awkward stage," her mother had insisted. "A stage when you have to struggle to get what you want. And do it on your own. It makes you appreciate everything more." She had hugged Melinda's thin shoulders as she said this.

But Melinda had disagreed silently, thinking, *It's better to be like Sharon.*

In her aunt's kitchen, Melinda struggled politely to take bites from a ham sandwich. Her stomach was empty, but clenched. Behind her, she heard a scraping sound; she turned and saw that on the kitchen counter was a metal cage; inside was a kitten-sized rodent with long fur and beady eyes. Sharon laughed at Melinda's expression. "Meet Festus," she said. "Mom's latest foster child from the pet store."

"He's been a little depressed, poor guy," Aunt Rita explained, tapping the side of the cage.

"Festus the pestus," Uncle Ted chimed in, coming back into the kitchen.

"Don't you want your sandwich?" Aunt Rita asked Melinda.

Sharon said, suddenly impatient, "I told you, Mother, she's too tired to eat! She needs to crash!"

"Of course she does," Aunt Rita said, getting up. "Let me help you get settled in for the night, Mindy."

"*I'll* do it, Mother," Sharon said pointedly.

Aunt Rita drew back, sat down again, her expression disappointed. But she said brightly, "Right, go ahead, you two. 'Night, Mindy."

Uncle Ted patted Melinda's shoulder as she passed. "I'll be better tomorrow," she promised them. She followed Sharon through a den filled with tropical aquariums and terrariums, up the stairs and past the two other bedrooms to a small guest room that Melinda remembered from other, brief visits. Two cats were curled together at the foot of the single guest bed—one, an orange tabby, had a splint on his rear paw. Sharon shooed them away and smoothed the bedspread. The room had only the bed, a nightstand, and a dresser. Her suitcases were on the floor. The walls were beige, the carpet beige, the ceiling off-white, the curtains a colorless gauze. It was a blank room, waiting to be filled. There were a dozen roses in a vase on the nightstand, the velvety blooms the only bright color in the room. Sharon gestured at them and rolled her eyes. "See what I mean? My mom stole those from my dad's garden. She's in hostess heaven."

A phone rang in the next room. Sharon jumped off the foot of the bed. "That's mine. Be right back."

Alone, Melinda unzipped the smaller suitcase, took out a new nightgown and put it on, moving slowly, like someone in a dream. She drifted into the bathroom, touching the walls as she walked, as if it was important not to move through this new space too quickly. Her face in the mirror was pale and exhausted, and even beyond that—different. She looked changed. She touched the sides of her face, staring into the mirror, and thought, *I did it. I left them.*

Sharon came back into the room, hugging herself. She spoke with little groaning noises around each word. "That was *him*. He just got back from Kalamazoo. He's the lead singer in a band, did I tell you? He was calling to tell me how much he misses me."

As Melinda climbed into bed, Sharon went on in a voice that seemed to be moving farther and farther away, "It's so incredible to feel this way about someone. I want to tell you all about him. I have so much to tell you. It's going to be such a perfect summer now."

Melinda whispered, "I have things to tell you, too."

She heard a more distant phone ringing below them, and remembered promising to call her mother as soon as she arrived. Aunt Rita's voice drifted up: "Mindy, it's your mother calling!"

Melinda didn't want to talk to her mother. She whispered to Sharon, "I can't get up."

"Want me to tell her you're already asleep?"

Melinda closed her eyes, nodding.

"And you'll call her in the morning?"

Melinda nodded again, barely. She was drifting away. Then, from somewhere inside herself, she found the strength to instruct, "Don't tell her I was crying."

"Our secret," Sharon said. She turned off Melinda's light. "Good-night, cousin Mindy," she called softly from the doorway. "Remember, you're free!"

TWO

❖

S he was used to having to figure out which bedroom she was in, in the first moments of waking. But this room was completely unfamiliar. *I'm at Sharon's,* she remembered. It made her instantly, anxiously wide awake, although it was very early; the clock beside her bed said six o'clock.

She sat up and looked around in the stillness. There was one window; it faced the street in front of the house and the eastern sky. The first peach-colored rays of dawn were coming over the roofs of the houses across the street. It was a quiet, tree-lined neighborhood unlike either of her own two neighborhoods—around her mother's apartment in Milwaukee or her father's farm. Melinda stood at the window a moment, feeling far away from everything familiar.

She wandered into the upstairs hallway. Framed family portraits hung against the faded flowery wallpaper; most were of Sharon, from birth to her sixteenth birthday, last year. Melinda gazed at them, admiring Sharon's unchangingly beautiful smile. But at the hallway's end, at the top of the stairs, there was an older photograph—black and white—that Melinda hadn't noticed before. It was a picture of her aunt and her mother as children, standing against a wooden fence. Aunt Rita was smiling at a kitten in her arms as it played with the end of one pigtail. Melinda's mother was leaning back, into the fence, her chin lifted, looking directly at the camera, but not exactly smiling. Her lips were curved, but it was more an expression of taking everything in, weighing it carefully.

Something brushed the hem of Melinda's nightgown, making her jump. It was the cat with the splinted paw, purring as he wove between her ankles. Melinda picked him up and rubbed his chin. When she set him back down, he limped through the partly open door of Sharon's bedroom and jumped to the foot of her bed. Melinda peeked in from the doorway.

The last time she'd seen Sharon's room, it had been peppermint pink with white furniture; now it was a bright, shimmery blue, the walls and ceiling like an upturned swimming pool, the pine floors strewn with brightly colored clothes. Melinda could see Sharon's auburn hair, tousled above the hem of a sky-blue comforter. *Sharon is here,* she remembered. *She's going to help me.*

It calmed her. She went back to her room and began to quietly unpack, putting the outfits in both suitcases into drawers or onto hangers. She had twice as many outfits as she needed, everything new and crisp and fashionable—polka dots and stripes and designer crests, clothes that her mother had bought for her and helped her to pack two nights ago. "Oh, my world traveler," her mother had sighed, laying the outfits expertly in Melinda's suitcase. "Ready to go off on your own and see the world?"

"I'm not going off to see the world," Melinda had insisted quietly. "I'm only going to Michigan."

Although now, in Michigan, it did feel as if she had come to a different world, a place too far away to come back from after the weekend, as she had always done, going back and forth between her mother's and her father's for as long as she could remember. In this place there would be no going back and forth, no transformation for the benefit of one parent or the other. Already she felt farther from them than she would ever have thought possible.

At the bottom of one suitcase, she found a pair of baggy khaki shorts and a plain white T-shirt. She put these on, brushed her hair, made her bed, and then lay back down on the bedspread until she heard the first sounds of the Parkers waking, the unfamiliar murmurings and creakings of a different family.

She let them all go downstairs first, listening and waiting, letting it sink in that this would be her family now.

"I hope we didn't wake you," Aunt Rita said. "Ted and I get up awfully early on Mondays. Ted's math class starts at eight o'clock and I go in to the shop first thing to make sure all my creatures survived the weekend."

"Even Sharon is up today, in your honor," Uncle Ted said, giving his daughter's arm a nudge. "Pass Melinda the muffins, you zombie."

Sharon gazed at Melinda sleepily, chin in hands, her

hair charmingly awry. She was wearing a black and white polka-dotted kimono. "Just don't expect me to do this every morning, okay?"

"She hasn't been up this early since school got out," Uncle Ted remarked.

Sharon made a face at him. "I had such a nice talk with your mom last night," she said to Melinda. "She's already started her workshop, did you know?"

Melinda nodded. "She left right after I did."

"I guess the first day went great. She sounded terrific. Imagine being one of the top speakers with all those TV news people. *Imagine*, Mom. Anyway, she left a number at the campus where you can call her today. She said to tell you she misses you like crazy already."

"I want to hear about your *dad*," Aunt Rita said curiously. She was wearing a different sweat suit this morning, this one baggy and blue with a large cowl that she hadn't rolled down yet; it circled her neck like a loose bandage. She was shoving chunks of carrot through the bars of the guinea pig's cage as she spoke. "Talk about somebody who's going to miss you! Did he really go all the way to England?"

"A week ago," Melinda said.

"Well, I hope he was in good physical shape," Uncle Ted remarked.

They all waited for him to explain. He said innocently, "Because now his money will turn into pounds!"

Sharon groaned, turned to Melinda, and went on, "It just doesn't sound like your dad—going to England! He's never done anything like this before, has he?"

"He got this grant from his college to study Shakespeare," Melinda said. "He said he never thought he'd get it. He said it would make him look bad with the department if he turned it down."

"Is it true that your stepmom went with him?" Aunt Rita asked.

"Alicia's been to England before. She's going to help him get used to it."

Aunt Rita's eyes widened over the tops of her glasses. "Alicia's been to England *before*?"

"Who'll take care of the chickens and goats?" Sharon wondered.

"A neighbor," Melinda explained. "And Alicia's coming back early. She just wanted to help Daddy get settled."

"Then he'll stay over there *alone*?" Aunt Rita asked, even more surprised.

Melinda was crumbling her muffin on her plate. The conversation was starting to unsettle her—having these relatives talk as if they knew her father. Her aunt was going on, "Well, people can change, you know. Maybe Steve will love London. Maybe he's not the stay-at-home we all thought he was."

"I think it's so cool," Sharon insisted. She mimicked a cultured voice. "Fah-thah is at Ox-ford for the suh-mah."

"I don't know why he went to England instead of Ireland," Uncle Ted said. "Ireland is the richest country in the world."

He waited for Melinda to raise her eyes and look at him. Then he exclaimed, "Because their capital is always Dublin!"

Sharon grumbled, "He actually inflicted that one on Evan last weekend."

"Yeah, and he loved it," Uncle Ted pronounced. "He almost cracked a real smile."

Before Sharon could retort, he leaned toward Melinda. "Say, I've got an idea for what we could all do together tonight. How does miniature golf sound to everybody?"

"I'm going over to Evan's tonight," Sharon protested quickly. "Remember I told you? We're working on his boat."

Uncle Ted put down his coffee slowly. "Sharon, in case it's slipped your mind, your favorite cousin arrived yesterday."

"No, I arranged this weeks ago!" Sharon insisted. "Remember, I mentioned it last weekend? Evan has to have his boat ready to sell by the end of the week. And I promised I'd help. He's counting on me!"

"Really, it's okay," Melinda said.

"See? Mindy doesn't mind."

Uncle Ted snapped open his newspaper. "Fine, we'll go golfing without you."

But Sharon turned next to her mother. "Don't make Mindy go miniature golfing, Mom! She's not eight years old, she's fifteen."

Melinda said, "I'll go. Really. It sounds fine."

Aunt Rita asked Sharon, "Sure you couldn't change your plans just for tonight?"

"Moth-er! I just *explained* why I can't."

"Who needs her?" Uncle Ted asked, his nose in the newspaper. Aunt Rita bit her lip and turned her attention back to the guinea pig.

When Melinda took her plate to the sink Sharon came up beside her, gave her a sympathetic look, and whispered, "Let's take a walk."

As they fell into step together on the shady sidewalk, Sharon apologized, "I did promise Evan that I'd help him." She added achingly, "And I haven't seen him in *three days*."

"We have lots of time," Melinda reminded her.

"I just wish you didn't have to go miniature golfing. Honestly, it's this form of torture they like to inflict on other people."

Melinda shrugged. She was used to having other people decide how she would spend her time, and besides, there was still the faint feeling of drifting, of being free. It didn't matter to her what she did. She looked around, trying to get a sense of place. Sharon's neighborhood was old-fashioned, the tree-lined streets fragrant, the houses old and close together, most painted white, all with pillared porches. Melinda had a scattering of memories of the last visits. "Isn't there a little store around the block there?" she asked Sharon, pointing ahead of them. "Where we bought some candy last time?"

Sharon nodded. "Mickey's. Pop and candy pit stop. Come on, I'll show you a shortcut." She gestured toward an overgrown paved path running between two houses on the other side of the street.

"Won't we be trespassing?" Melinda asked.

"Everybody uses it," Sharon assured her. "This isn't Milwaukee, Mindy—you're in rinky-town now."

As they passed the house nearest to the shortcut, Sharon waved to someone sitting on the porch, a hazy figure behind a sheen of sunlit screen. "How's it going, Paul?" she called, her voice bright, insistent. She steered Melinda closer. "This is my cousin Mindy from Milwaukee."

"Hi, Mindy from Milwaukee," a voice replied, not particularly friendly.

They kept walking. The shortcut was almost like a tunnel, with mock orange bushes arching over their heads and overgrown cement circles at their feet. They emerged into a narrow alley; Mickey's was to the right. Sharon pointed to the store. "Need pop or anything now?"

Melinda shook her head. "Let's walk around the block. I want to get used to your neighborhood."

"Get used to the boredom, you mean. Nothing ever happens here. I'd be out of my mind this summer if I hadn't met Evan at the Riverwatch. That's where I'm waitressing this summer. Evan's band plays every other weekend. They're fantastic—they'll be famous soon, I'm sure of it. They're called the Con-Artists, after Evan's last name—O'Connor. Isn't that cool?"

Melinda nodded.

"Did I tell you how we met? One Friday night, I'd just finished my shift at the Riverwatch and I was sitting at a table with a couple of the other waitresses and Evan sat down with us and just started *talking*, I swear to God. I don't even remember what we were talking about, but pretty soon he was just talking to *me* and it was like we already knew each other. It was like this powerful connection, like we were on the exact same wavelength. Instantly! A few weeks later, he asked me out. Naturally Mom and Pops completely freaked when they first met him because he's a little older than what they're used to, but Mindy—wait until you see him. He's gorgeous."

But then she scowled. "Did you notice how they reacted when I said I was seeing him tonight? Like it was some big personal letdown for them? They do that to me every single time I go out with him. I just hate it when they treat me like I'm still their little possession! God, Mindy, at least *your* parents are used to the idea of not having you around them every minute. You are so lucky."

Lucky? Melinda thought, shocked. *How could you think I'm lucky?* Something came to her, a feeling that she had been in a conversation with Sharon that had taken this turn before. She shook her head free of it and managed to say, "It isn't really like that . . ."

But Sharon was still talking. "My parents would *never* let me go anywhere for the summer. Do you know I've never been away from home longer than a week at Girl Scout camp? I honestly don't know how they're going to handle me going away to college. They act like it's a family crisis if I have two dates in the same weekend!"

"It isn't really like that," Melinda said more insistently.

Sharon looked puzzled. "Like what?"

"What you said about my parents being used to me being away. They aren't."

"Mindy, they'd have to be! You've been going back and forth since you were a baby."

"But the thing is, they still fight about it. And I end up feeling guilty all the time."

"*Tell* me about feeling guilty! The guilt trips are driving me crazy! No wonder we end up losing our tempers all the time!"

"I never do that," Melinda said softly.

Sharon didn't hear. She was shaking her head at the aggravation of it all. "God, I'm so glad you're here. I won't have to feel so alone with them. And they'll be nice to you, they'll let you do whatever you want because you're company."

Anything I want, Melinda thought. It was so unusual for her to think that way—she didn't even really know what it meant. But she smiled at Sharon and Sharon put an arm around her waist, giving her an encouraging hug as they walked. They came back up the porch steps that way, but Melinda turned slightly before they went back inside and saw Paul, standing on the steps outside his porch. He had half turned, too; he was looking over his shoulder at them. When he caught Melinda's eye, he looked away quickly, but not before Melinda had seen a pained expression cross his face.

The golf course was called Yogi Bear's Funland, with a ten-foot-high statue of Yogi in the parking lot, grinning at people as they pulled in. Most of the golfers were parents with small children, but Melinda wasn't embarrassed to be there. No one knew her; she felt invisible. And besides, it was so different to be with her aunt and uncle. They weren't acting like typical adults; they teased and pushed and bumped hips with each other. Melinda watched her aunt with particular curiosity, trying to make sense of the fact that this was her mother's only sister—this plump, round-shouldered, giggling woman in faded stretch denims, a red bandanna covering her frizzy hair.

She was the worst golfer Melinda had ever seen. She broke up laughing every time she raised her club to hit the ball because she knew in advance how badly she would miss. The fact that she was enjoying this incompetence surprised Melinda—it was such a contrast to her own mother, who hated to do anything badly. Halfway through the course Uncle Ted started yelling for the golfers at nearby holes to duck and cover their heads. By the end of the game, Melinda was giggling helplessly, too.

Aunt Rita took her aside and said, "Just humor us for a few more minutes and then we'll take you for ice cream."

From the backseat of the car, Melinda watched her aunt and uncle grin at each other. "You didn't disappoint me, Rita," Uncle Ted said. "Your game is as unconventional as ever."

"Thank you, Arnold Palmer," Aunt Rita said. She turned and asked Melinda, "Was I that bad?"

"Maybe you should try bowling," Melinda said. "They use a bigger ball."

They laughed approvingly. "You and your mom ever play miniature golf in Milwaukee?" Uncle Ted asked.

"Liz play miniature golf?" Aunt Rita exclaimed. "You think my sister would even consider playing a sport that involved artificial grass and little plastic bridges?"

Melinda didn't know what to say to this. "She started jogging this year," she offered.

"Did she?" Aunt Rita asked. "Oh dear, I should start jogging too, before I get any fatter. Maybe I could jog to work?"

"It might be a little hard, running with those gerbil cages under your arms," Uncle Ted said.

Aunt Rita went on, "Did you know that in high school Liz was captain of the volleyball team? Our team was state champions two years in a row, did she tell you that? She was good at so many things, your mom. So sharp and full of determination. Sometimes it was impossible to feel like she was the little sister."

Melinda listened, trying to imagine her mother as anyone's little sister.

"And she went away to college when she was only seventeen—skipped senior year and everything. Me, I still hadn't figured out what to do with myself at that point—I was working in a grocery store—but Liz knew. And she was in a big hurry to get where people would finally appreciate her."

"Didn't people appreciate her in Wisconsin?"

Aunt Rita sighed. "We grew up in such a small town, honey. And our parents were pretty old-fashioned, as I'm sure you've noticed. They just didn't understand how badly she needed to break away."

Uncle Ted said, "Well, people appreciate her now, don't they, Mindy? Top-notch anchorwoman in Milwaukee. Pretty impressive, I'd say."

He pulled off the highway to a drive-in and ordered three chocolate milk shakes. When he handed Melinda hers, he announced, "Old Sharon will never know what she missed tonight, will she, Mindy?"

Melinda nodded and sipped the milk shake gratefully—the perfect thing for her still jittery stomach. Aunt Rita confided, her voice suddenly unmistakably sad, "We can't help missing her, can we, Ted? She used to get so excited about a stupid golf game. Remember? Remember how careful we had to be to let her win?"

Melinda heard Uncle Ted's hand sliding across the front seat, toward Aunt Rita's. They looked at each other. For a long, embarrassed moment, Melinda wondered if they were about to kiss. But instead Uncle Ted put his hands on the wheel, started up the car, and drove them home.

THREE

❖

"Y ou don't have to make my breakfast," Melinda told her aunt the next morning. "I can just get myself some cereal."

Aunt Rita turned from the stove, disappointed. "Oh, let me make you an omelet—please? I love making omelets and nobody here eats eggs anymore."

"If you're sure you have enough time before work," Melinda said.

"No problem at all," Aunt Rita insisted, whisking eggs happily. "I'll just whip up an omelet for you and then I have to stop at the supermarket, pick up some fresh greens for our new lop-eared rabbits. We got half a dozen of them last week. They are so adorable! If you'd like, you could come with me and—"

She stopped herself. "Oh, never mind, you have better things to do this morning."

"I'll come," Melinda said. "I'm all dressed and everything and Sharon is still asleep."

"You wouldn't mind? We can pick up a few groceries

too, while we're out. I don't really know what kind of snacks you like to have around."

The back of Aunt Rita's station wagon was piled with assorted animal cages and bags of litter and feed. "Do you bring animals home from your store a lot?" Melinda asked.

"Now and then, when they need a little extra TLC. I may have to bring home a lop-ear next; I have one on a hunger strike already. But we'll try the Boston lettuce cure first."

In the supermarket, she headed straight for the produce section, Melinda following with the cart. "I should make a pot of vegetable soup," Aunt Rita announced, looking around. "Would you like some homemade soup for lunch?"

"What about work?" Melinda asked.

"Oh, they can manage without me one morning. I'll drop the lettuce off—my assistant can feed the rabbits. I'm really in the mood to make soup. Pick out some snacks for yourself and we'll head back."

Melinda picked out olives and water biscuits and smoked oysters, a favorite snack at her mother's. Aunt Rita shook her head when she saw them in the cart. "I can sure tell whose daughter you are. Your mother used to eat the strangest things. Even as a kid, pickles and olives and dried figs, when the rest of us were hoarding candy."

"I like hearing you talk about my mother," Melinda told her aunt when they were back in the car.

Aunt Rita smiled. "Having you here is bringing back a lot of sisterly memories. I'm so glad you decided to come stay with us instead of going to Grandma's."

"I thought about it," Melinda told her. "My mom thought coming here would be a little too far. But I wanted to be with Sharon."

"Of course you did," Aunt Rita agreed. "My folks like all that northern woods solitude, but Perkinstown is no place for a teenager in the summer. Take it from somebody who grew up there."

Melinda nodded. "My mom says it was pretty boring."

"She was a big-city person, even before she'd ever been to one," Aunt Rita agreed.

"Sometimes I feel so different from my mom. And other times I feel like we're almost like sisters."

Aunt Rita's smile wavered when she heard this. She had pulled the car to a stop in front of the Magic Kingdom Pet Store and seemed suddenly preoccupied, gathering up her bags of lettuce, her pocketbook, kitty litter and bird feed. "Come in for a minute, if you want to see our rabbits."

Melinda followed her past tanks and cages, empty and full. The shop was filled with frantic, ear-piercing yowling, coming from the back of the store. "A Siamese kitten," Aunt Rita explained on their way back to the car. "A real handful. Hope I don't have to bring *that* monster home."

Melinda wanted to continue their conversation. "Do you sometimes feel like you and Sharon are like sisters?" she asked as soon as they were back in the car.

Aunt Rita looked out the window a moment. Finally she answered, "Oh, I used to. But that can only go so far." Her expression changed, grew more impatient. "And now of course it's all Evan, Evan, Evan." She frowned, started up the car, and drove them home.

Sharon was sitting at the kitchen table with a plate of toast. "Your mom called again," she announced. "I looked all over for you. Where did you guys go?"

"Give her a call back now," Aunt Rita instructed, taking the grocery bag from Melinda's arms. "If you need privacy, take the phone from the den and plug it in upstairs."

Melinda got the phone and carried it upstairs. But alone in the guest room, she couldn't bring herself to dial the number. After a few minutes, she took the phone back downstairs. "There was no answer," she told her aunt. "I'll try again tonight."

Aunt Rita nodded, chopping carrots and celery. "Sharon's on the porch—go ahead and join her. It's turning into such a beautiful day."

Sharon was stretched out in the lounger; Melinda sat on the porch swing. "Mom sure is in a good mood," Sharon observed. "What did you two do?"

"Bought lettuce for the rabbits." Melinda giggled.

"Thrill of a lifetime. I can't believe she's actually making soup for us. Pops and I are always kidding her about how she won't cook for us anymore because we aren't animals." She looked out into the street and lowered her voice. "There's Paul again."

She sent him a little wave. He didn't wave back. "Oh, be that way," she scolded softly. She put her lounger back another notch and smiled up at Melinda. "Well, here we are, Cousin. Your second big day in picturesque St. Joseph. And you've already been to Yogi Bear's Funland and the Magic Kingdom Pet Store. Are you surviving the excitement?"

"So far so good."

"Well, tell me all about your life these days. What's new? Any serious crushes? Who's your best friend? Didn't you say in your letter that your best friend is into ballet?"

Melinda hesitated. Connie wasn't her friend anymore; they hadn't even spoken since early spring. The friendship had taken a familiar turn—an intense, hopeful beginning and then Melinda started pulling away, uncomfortable about bringing anyone into her double life, her separate homes. She had cut Connie off in midfriendship, avoiding her at school, ignoring her calls, and no one had replaced her.

"It didn't work out with Connie," she told Sharon. "We didn't have anything in common."

"It sounded like you did, in your letter."

Melinda chose her words carefully. "Sometimes it's hard for me to get close to other people with the way I live. You know. The way things are."

Sharon looked puzzled.

"Having divorced parents and going back and forth and everything," Melinda explained.

"But lots of my friends' parents are divorced," Sharon insisted. "And this is a small town. There must be tons of kids where you live who would understand. And they would think it's cool that you have two different homes."

Melinda looked away, trying to push back the vague memory of an earlier, similar conversation. She saw movement on the porch across the street, Paul going back inside his house. "Are you still friends with him?" she asked, pointing to where he had been sitting.

"Oh, Paul. I've known him since we were both in kindergarten. But now I think he's mad at me. I don't know why. Maybe because I never introduced him to Evan. Who, by the way, I'll be introducing *you* to tonight."

Melinda was still gazing around the neighborhood, trying to collect her thoughts.

"Did you hear what I said?" Sharon asked.

"Sorry. I was just thinking about how different your neighborhood is from either of mine."

"Which home will you miss the most?" Sharon asked, as if it was a quiz question.

Melinda admitted softly, "I don't know."

"It'll probably be equal," Sharon decided for her. "Since both places are so different. So did you hear what I said about tonight?"

"What's happening tonight?" Aunt Rita asked, coming out onto the porch. She was wearing her pet-store smock: bright pink with silk-screened goldfish and parakeets.

"I asked Evan to bring me home from work and have dinner with us," Sharon told her. "So he can meet Mindy."

Aunt Rita said mildly, "Glad you mentioned it. Soup's on the stove, girls. Enjoy your lunch. I have to get to work."

When she had driven away, Melinda felt a sudden need to be alone. "Think I'll try calling my mom again," she told Sharon.

At the top of the stairs, she passed the photo of the sisters, took it off the wall, carried it to her room and let the memory come.

It was the time her aunt, her uncle, and Sharon had come to Milwaukee, five years ago—arriving unannounced after a funeral in Chicago. It was a Friday and Melinda always went to her father's on Fridays. When her mother called him to ask if Melinda could stay with her, at least until Saturday, Melinda watched her mother's expression change, heard her voice sharpen. "And I suppose that it's too earthshaking to be put off one week, is that it? Some chicken might lay an extra egg or something?"

Melinda looked sideways at Sharon, embarrassed. Sharon whispered pleadingly, "If you go, take me with you. Don't leave me alone with them, I'll *die*."

"You want to come to my dad's?" Melinda repeated.

"We'll beg them until they say yes. But act like it was your idea or else my mom will get mad at me for inviting myself."

When her father said yes, Melinda suspected that Alicia had intervened. Alicia was always asking Melinda to bring a friend to the farm, but Melinda had never found the right person to bring, the one who would really understand and appreciate her other world. Now, miraculously, there was Sharon. "Is it a real farm?" Sharon asked. "I mean, your dad's not exactly a farmer type. Do they just call it a farm because it's out in the country?"

"It's real," Melinda said. "Alicia's the farmer."

"It's not a cattle ranch, Sharon, if that's what you're looking for," her mother added. She was angry that Melinda wasn't staying in the city. "I'll drive the girls," she told Aunt Rita and Uncle Ted. "There's no point in dragging everybody out to the middle of nowhere."

"All I have with me are dress-up clothes," Sharon complained. "I didn't bring anything farm-ish."

Melinda said, "Don't worry, we'll share my clothes." It was back in the days when they were more or less the same size.

"You have clothes already there?" Sharon asked, then answered herself, "Of course you do! Stupid me. You have a whole bedroom there! Wow, is it as fancy as your bedroom here?"

"It's different," Melinda told her, then added, breathless with excitement, "you'll see."

And from her first glimpse of the property, Sharon did see. "A real barn!" she'd cried, pointing to it from the backseat of Melinda's mother's Volvo as they pulled into the spruce-lined driveway. And then, even more amazed, "There's a goat in your barn!" She started bouncing up and down on the seat. As soon as the car came to a stop, she threw open the door and raced toward the enormous bleached barn. Melinda and her mother smiled at each other. "She's probably never been to a farm before," Melinda said.

"Keep an eye on her," her mother said. "And take it easy on poor Alicia. Don't make more work for her, she has enough on her hands."

"We won't," Melinda promised.

Alicia had come to the back door then, wearing a carpenter's apron over her faded jeans. She and Melinda's mother waved at each other politely, briefly. Melinda left the car, but blew her mother a reassuring kiss as the Volvo backed out of the driveway. Then she ran after Sharon, who was running back out of the barn, a brown egg in each hand.

Alicia was charmed by Sharon's excitement; she gave her a thorough tour of the property, showing her the chickens, the goats, the apple orchard, the elaborate garden, the pottery shed full of baked and unbaked pots. But Melinda noticed her father's uneasiness. He was quiet around Sharon and very formal. It made her feel torn.

At the dinner table, Sharon's questions were unstoppable. "How long have you had this place, Uncle Steve?" she asked, buttering a thick slice of Alicia's homemade bread.

"I inherited the farm when I lost my parents. I had just graduated from college and the last thing I was expecting to own was a farm." He smiled meaningfully at Alicia. "But now I can't imagine living anywhere else."

"Did you intend to be a farmer?" Sharon asked Alicia.

"As a child, I used to dream of living on a farm," Alicia told her. "And the very first time I saw this place, I knew I'd found my soul home. Do you know what a soul home is, Sharon? It's the home you're born for. The place you truly belong."

Melinda had heard all this before; she wasn't sure she liked Alicia telling Sharon. It was too much of a secret, this love the three of them shared for the farm. Sometimes to her mother, she complained about the weekends, said they were boring, because she sensed that her mother needed to believe that Melinda didn't really belong there. But secretly, she treasured every wild acre of it.

"Personally, I don't think I could handle living here all the time," Sharon was saying. "I'd miss my friends too much. Nobody to ride bikes with and that kind of thing."

"Sometimes a place can be a friend," Melinda's father interjected. "Right, Linda?"

Sharon laughed, as if he'd told a joke. "How can you ride bikes with a place?" She asked Melinda, "Can we go up in the hayloft now?"

Melinda took her up the ladder to the very top of the barn and showed her a tunnel she'd made of stacked bales of hay. At the end of this tunnel was a small, round window, through which they could see clear to the far edges of the property. "This is my favorite place of all," she confessed.

"It's the greatest," Sharon agreed. "You can see the whole world from up here. I *love* this farm."

"You do?"

"Oh, *sure*. I'd love to be able to come here. Once a month would be about perfect. Like just when I was starting to get too hassled at one home, I could cut out to the other!"

She lay back in the hay, wearing a pair of Melinda's old overalls, chewing a straw. "Your dad is really serious, isn't he, Mindy? I don't mean he's not okay—he's nice. And your stepmom is too. But they're kind of like hippies, aren't they? Earthy types."

Melinda cringed protectively. "My dad's not a hippie," she said quietly.

"Oh, you know what I mean. And I love the way they both call you Linda! I've never thought of you as a Linda, but you know, out here it kind of fits you. You seem a little different. It would be kind of neat to have two names. Maybe while I'm here, you should call me Sherry. Or Cher."

Melinda was looking out the tiny window, feeling confused.

Sharon continued philosophically, "To tell you the truth, Mindy, I can see why your mom didn't last out here very long."

Melinda turned from the window to look at her. "What do you mean?"

"I was just thinking about all that soul-home stuff your stepmom was saying. I mean, your mom would never choose this place for a soul home. She's too glamorous. She's involved in too many things. One time I overheard my mom telling my dad that she knew from day one the marriage wouldn't last. She said she was surprised it even lasted a year."

Melinda had never heard anyone talk this way about her parents' marriage. She felt a painful surge of curiosity. "So what else did your mom say?" she asked carefully.

Sharon thought a moment. "She said that your mom refused to talk about it. Man, if my mom and dad ever split up, I would demand to know every single detail. I would say: give me a *hundred* good reasons or I'll never speak to either one of you—"

"I was a baby," Melinda interrupted.

"What?"

"I was still a baby, how could I demand anything?"

"Right, but that was *good*. Because now it's all worked out, everybody is used to it and you have a fantastic apartment in Milwaukee and this great farm and two of everything and parents who are always trying to outdo each other." She giggled. "You are so lucky."

Melinda looked out the window again, into the bleached wheatfields, where the sun was going down. She wished Sharon would stop talking, but Sharon was rambling on, "Two different houses. Two different bedrooms. Different parties. Different clothes. Even *you* seem different. Don't you miss your friends when you're out here, though? Oh, but wait, this would be a fantastic place to bring friends! You could have big slumber parties, right here in this hayloft—"

"We'd better go in," Melinda interrupted.

"Not yet," Sharon protested. "I love it up here."

"There are a lot of spiders, they come out at night."

"Let's go watch TV," Sharon suggested, standing up and dusting off her overalls. "I was just about to ask you if your dad has a TV. He seems like the type who wouldn't have one."

"We watch TV here all the time," Melinda insisted. Which wasn't true.

The rest of the weekend passed quickly; Alicia filled the hours with pottery making and cooking and farm chores. She showed Sharon how to milk the goat, how to knead bread dough, how to tie up tomato plants in the garden. Sharon enjoyed everything, but Melinda was now waiting for the weekend to end; she was anxious to have the farm to herself again. She could tell that her father was, too.

On Sunday afternoon, when her mother's horn honked from the driveway, she and her father looked at each other, a private glance of relief.

"Will you invite me again?" Sharon asked on her way out the door.

Alicia laughed at her boldness. "Sharon, you are welcome anytime. I mean it, standing invitation."

Melinda sent her father another furtive look of reassurance: *I won't invite her.* He squeezed Melinda's hand. In the car, Sharon told Melinda's mother, "We had the greatest time, Aunt Liz, it's like another world out here."

"Isn't it though?" Melinda's mother agreed dryly. She told Sharon, "Your mother and father missed you terribly."

Hearing this, Sharon rolled her eyes at Melinda. "Like I was gone a month." She reported to her aunt, "Mindy's stepmom said I could come back anytime I want."

"Did she? She probably appreciated the stimulation."

"I can't wait to go back," Sharon said. She turned to Melinda. "Let's spend a whole vacation out there someday."

"Someday," Melinda echoed vaguely. She could have arranged it for the very next summer, if she'd wanted to. Even her father wouldn't have refused. But she had never asked for it and so it had never happened again.

Now in the Parker guest bed, she asked herself, *Did I always do that? Keep people away?*

Sharon's voice came to her from the next room, interrupting her thoughts, its sweetness changing, climbing in pitch and volume. She was talking on the phone and something was wrong. "Why can't you just start practice a few hours later? I already told everyone you'd be here! What difference would it make to just start a little *later*?"

Then silence. Then, after a few moments, a knock on Melinda's door. "Come in," Melinda called.

"I have to go to work now," Sharon announced. She was wearing shiny black pants, a white shirt, and a black bow tie, frowning and picking cat hairs off the front of her pants. "Look, would you do me a favor and tell my mom that Evan and I won't be able to make it for dinner? We'll stop by for a few minutes afterwards so that you two can still meet each other. Okay, Mindy?"

"Okay, sure," Melinda said. She hesitated, but then asked, "Is everything all right?"

"Oh, Evan scheduled a practice for tonight, he forgot about coming over. He's so busy lately with the band. They're getting all this attention from people out of town. Evan's actually planning to take the Con-Artists to Chicago in the fall, see if he can get something started with a manager over there."

"You mean move away?"

Sharon nodded sadly. "It's not a surprise. I've known it all along. It's the reason why this summer is so precious. Anyway, I have to go, I'm late for work. Tell Mom we'll stop by around seven, okay?"

Melinda stood at her window, watching Sharon walk to her car. Suddenly she felt intensely lonely. She heard music coming faintly from across the street, a reggae beat, drifting to her window from Paul's porch. Paul was there. He stood up as Sharon drove away, craning his neck and frowning. He was watching her, too.

Melinda was eating a bowl of Aunt Rita's soup on the front porch when the mailman came. She took the bundle of mail he handed her and saw right away the blue airmail letter on the top, addressed to her. Her heart constricted. She stared at it in her lap a few moments before she opened it.

Dear Linda,

On Sunday I spent the entire day imagining you on your train ride to St. Joseph. I hope you felt my concern for you, propelling you to your safe destination. It seemed strange to be an ocean away from you while you were yourself traveling and I was relieved when the day was over and I knew that you had arrived. Alicia says it's good that we are both breaking new ground this summer, but I can't help feeling that this is too much, that it doesn't make sense to be so far away from you and for you to be so far away from me and from the apartment as well.

Melinda stopped reading. She felt disappointed in her father, both for sounding so morose and for not mentioning her mother by her name. He had described her journey to St. Joseph as though it were space travel, involving no people.

By the time you get this letter, you will have spent the first days of your summer in St. Joseph. I certainly hope you are making good use of your time. Be sure to sign up for something that will challenge your mind and keep expanding your horizons.

Melinda put the letter down and closed her eyes tightly. When she opened them she saw that from across the street, Paul was waving at her. She waved back uncertainly. He waved again, more insistently, and she realized that he was inviting her over. She got up and crossed the street slowly, the envelope still in her hand.

He was sitting on his front steps, wearing baggy shorts and a tank top; the outfit made him look all arms and legs. A pair of reflector sunglasses hid his eyes. Melinda stood in front of him for a moment, shifting her weight around, and then asked, finally, "Well?"

"Well, what?"

"Well, what do you *want*?"

He stalled, then pointed to the letter in her hand. "News from Milwaukee?" he asked.

She shook her head. "My dad is in London."

"Cool," he said. "Why are you stuck here?"

His tone annoyed her. "I'm not *stuck* here."

He looked unconvinced. "You wouldn't rather be in London?"

Melinda hesitated. "It's complicated."

"Naturally." He waited.

"My dad is in London for the summer," Melinda reported uncertainly. "Ordinarily he lives on a farm outside of Milwaukee. And my mom lives in the city."

Paul took off his shades and raised his bushy eyebrows. "Does this mean Mindy from Milwaukee is one of those children of divorce?" Challenging her, to see if she could handle it.

Melinda replied, equally sarcastic, "Yes, I'm from a broken home."

Paul grinned approvingly. He jerked his thumb over his shoulder, toward his front door. "My family's nuclear. Totally overrated. You an only child?"

"Just me. You too?"

"Might as well be. My sister's way older. So are you here because your parents split up?"

Melinda shook her head. "They did it a long time ago. I was a baby."

"Really?" he asked. He pondered this for a moment. "Don't all the big experts say that that's the best scenario? Having your folks split up before you're old enough to know what's going on?"

Melinda looked away. "I don't know what all the big experts say."

"Anyway, why are you so bummed out?"

"I'm not *bummed out*."

"Yes, you are. I could tell from clear across the street."

Melinda crossed her arms in annoyance and the letter fell from her hand. Paul picked it up for her, glancing at it before she snatched it back. "Why is it addressed to a Linda Morrison?" he asked.

"Because that's me," Melinda said. "My dad calls me Linda."

"You mean your dad calls you Linda and your mom calls you Mindy?" Paul exclaimed. "Not *too* schizy. Will the real daughter please stand up?"

This embarrassed Melinda. She blushed and turned away.

"Wait, I'm an impartial bystander. Which one is it? What should I call you—Mindy or Linda?"

Melinda thought about it. "You can call me Melinda."

"Hmmm," he observed. "Kind of stuffy."

Melinda drew back, insulted. But then she asked, challenging him, "So how long have you been hung up on my cousin?"

His expression changed. He looked stung.

"Don't worry," Melinda added, "she doesn't know."

He put his shades back on and announced, "She doesn't know, because she doesn't *care*." He stood up without another word and went back inside his house.

FOUR

❖

"Knock, knock," Uncle Ted said at the dinner table, smiling at Melinda.

"Who's there," Melinda said dutifully.

"Rigor," Uncle Ted said.

"Rigor, who?"

"Rigor Mortis, may I set in?"

Melinda laughed aloud at this one. But Aunt Rita said gently, "No jokes around Evan tonight, okay, Ted?"

"I thought you said he wasn't coming!"

"He's not coming for *dinner*," Aunt Rita explained. "But he is stopping in with Sharon to meet Mindy. Maybe they'll stay for dessert. I made something special this afternoon." She beamed at Melinda. "I remembered that a certain niece of mine has a favorite kind of pie."

Melinda asked hopefully, "Lemon meringue?"

Aunt Rita took a pie with an impressive-looking crown of meringue out of the refrigerator and held it aloft for them to admire. "How do you rate, Mindy?" Uncle Ted grumbled good-naturedly. "This woman hasn't made a pie for me in years."

"Oh, don't exaggerate!" Aunt Rita scolded. She lifted and aimed the pie at him.

"She's guilty of carrying a congealed weapon!" Uncle Ted exclaimed.

"I decided something today," Melinda interrupted them. "I think from now on, I'd like to be called Melinda instead of Mindy."

"I'd be happy to call you Melinda," Aunt Rita said. "It's a beautiful name."

"You're the boss," Uncle Ted said. "Remind me if I forget a few times." Melinda agreed, marveling at their acceptance. Her mother would have teased her, her father would have asked a dozen questions about the state of mind that had brought this on.

Aunt Rita was sectioning the pie when they heard the front door open and close. Sharon came sailing into the kitchen, leading Evan by the hand, smiling from ear to ear. "Here we are!" she sang. She pointed to Melinda and said, "Mindy, Evan; Evan, Mindy."

Aunt Rita said helpfully, "Mindy just told us that she'd prefer to be called Melinda from now on."

"Really?" Sharon asked. She nodded at Melinda. "I totally approve. It sounds so much more sophisticated." She corrected her introduction. "Evan O'Connor, this is my cousin, Melinda Morrison."

"Hey, Melinda," Evan said breezily. Melinda said hello back, trying to keep her voice normal. He was so handsome, a movie-star kind of handsome, with white-blond hair in a ponytail and a diamond in one ear. His eyes were china blue. Sharon hung on one suntanned arm, smiling up at him.

"Would you two care for some dessert?" Aunt Rita asked primly, breaking the silence. She pointed to the pie.

Sharon hesitated, but Evan said to her, "We have time, kid, let's have some pie."

Uncle Ted pulled up a chair for each of them. "Did you finish fixing up your boat last night?" he asked Evan.

"All finished," Evan replied. "Now it looks so beautiful I kind of hate to sell it. But I really need the money if I'm ever gonna get this band of mine to Chicago."

"Still planning on the fall?" Uncle Ted asked.

"Right," Evan said. "We've already had a few calls from Chicago managers, interested in hearing our demo."

"Evan, that's wonderful," Aunt Rita said. "We've heard such good things about your band from Sharon."

But Sharon was frowning, her head lowered. She asked, "Could we please not talk about Evan leaving?"

Evan had turned his attention to Melinda. "Did I hear you're from Milwaukee?" he asked. "What sort of a music scene do they have around there—is it anything like Chicago?"

Melinda shrugged apologetically. "I don't really know."

"She's young for the music scene," Aunt Rita pointed out.

"Not like our little barfly, here," Uncle Ted interjected, gesturing at Sharon.

Sharon fidgeted, annoyed.

"Evan, more pie?" Aunt Rita asked. The first piece had disappeared.

"Evan has a practice," Sharon announced, standing up.

"I'm going to listen for just a little while—maybe an hour or so—then I'll come back and we can do something all together, okay? Watch a video or something?"

As soon as they were gone, Aunt Rita and Uncle Ted looked at each other, disappointed. "Do you think she'll really be back in an hour?" Aunt Rita asked.

"Should I really rent a video?"

Aunt Rita shrugged. "Oh, why not? Get something cheerful for Mindy. I mean, Melinda."

"How about a nice teen romance?" Uncle Ted suggested glumly.

Melinda helped her aunt carry dishes from the table to the sink. "You don't like Evan, do you?" she asked.

"We think he's too old for Sharon," Aunt Rita confessed. "Did she tell you, he's twenty-three? I don't know, maybe I'm not being fair, but, I mean, the last boy Sharon dated wore *braces*, you know?"

"You mean Paul?" Melinda asked.

"Oh, I'd forgotten about Paul," Aunt Rita admitted. "I don't think that was ever anything serious, although he's a great kid. But I can't help feeling like Evan's changed Sharon. She's either in a state of absolute bliss or a state of utter despair. It's so hard for me to watch her taking this completely temporary relationship so seriously."

"At least he's leaving," Melinda reminded her.

"September," Aunt Rita agreed, holding up crossed fingers. She put the last of the dishes into the dishwasher and dried her hands. "Now," she said. "Let's cheer up and feed the fish."

Melinda followed her into the den and watched her sprinkle flakes into her three aquariums, crooning at the darting tropical fish. "Aunt Rita," she asked, "you know that picture of you and my mom at the top of the stairs? Do you have any other ones like that?"

Aunt Rita put the fish food container down, surprised and pleased. "What a coincidence that you would ask me that! Because just last night I got this unexplainable urge to look at old pictures. And I found an album at the back of my closet with some wonderful pictures of Liz. Wait right here—I'll get it for you."

She ran up the stairs and came back down with a faded maroon album. They sat down together on the sofa, the album in their laps. "I'm afraid there aren't many. My folks hardly ever took pictures. But there might be a few things here that you haven't seen before."

There were. In most of them, Melinda's mother was a blond teenager, tall and elegant, always with the same cautious half-smile. "Liz always looked older than me," Aunt Rita said. "Since birth, I think. I was stuck with the baby face."

It was true—Aunt Rita did always look younger, with her round, freckled face and full-cheeked smile. "You were really cute, though," Melinda said. Her mother looked too tall and serious to ever be called cute.

She turned the page and a loose photograph fell out of the book, against her leg. It was a picture of her father and mother and herself together. Her mother was dressed uncharacteristically in jeans and a man's cardigan, her blond hair pulled forward over one shoulder in a loose braid. Her father's hair was dark, shoulder-length, and unkempt, like Melinda's in the mornings. Melinda was a baby, standing between her seated parents; they each steadied a leg with one hand. Her mother was looking up at Melinda, smiling proudly. Her father was looking at the camera, his expression uncertain, as if he was wondering how in the world he'd come to be where he was.

"I'd forgotten about this one," Aunt Rita reported softly. "It was taken right here in St. Joseph, on our front porch here—see the porch swing? The only time Liz and Steve left the farm together while they were married. I begged her to come visit me and she finally did."

"Why only once?"

Aunt Rita hesitated, choosing her words carefully. "Your mother was trying very hard. Giving the marriage everything she had. You know the way she is, she doesn't often change her mind. I guess it was easier to just stay put ... until ... until she was sure ... about ... leaving."

There was a short silence. "I can't picture my mother on a farm," Melinda said finally.

Aunt Rita agreed softly, "Neither could we."

"Why do you think she married him in the first place?"

Aunt Rita looked at her. "She was in love with him, honey."

"In love?" Melinda repeated disbelievingly.

"Of course she was. They were both in love. And he was lost by himself on that farm. Look, I know that Liz doesn't like to talk about this, but don't you have pictures like this, of all three of you together?"

Melinda shook her head. "Neither of them kept any."

"Well, you can keep this one, if you want it."

Melinda said, trying to sound nonchalant, "Hmmm. Maybe I'll just take it upstairs for a while."

"Keep it, Melinda. It's yours."

Melinda turned the photograph over in her hand.

There was handwriting on the back; she recognized her mother's elegant script: *Our trip to St. Joseph. Melinda Catherine gives me hope.* She turned it back over again, sitting very still, fighting tears.

Uncle Ted came back in from the video store. "I got a comedy," he said. "It's supposed to be 'uplifting and hilarious.'"

Aunt Rita scoffed. "They all say that, Ted."

They put it on without waiting for Sharon. Melinda sat on the couch between them, holding the photograph, glancing at it from time to time. She couldn't really concentrate on the movie, but it helped to sit with her aunt and uncle; it soothed her. And she could tell that she was helping them, keeping them from being disappointed in Sharon, who didn't come back in an hour, as she'd promised, or even two hours. When the movie ended, Melinda said good-night to her aunt and uncle, took the photograph to her room, and put it on her nightstand.

FIVE

* ❖ *

When the telephone rang, Aunt Rita gave Melinda a guilty look across the breakfast table. "I'll bet I know who that is."

"I forgot to call her last night," Melinda said.

Aunt Rita picked up the phone on the second ring and began immediately to apologize. "I know, I know, Liz—she did try yesterday, right after you called. Yes, but things can get pretty zooey around here, as you know. Hang on a second, she just came down for breakfast."

She covered the receiver and whispered, "I'll take my coffee out to the porch." Then she handed Melinda the phone and left the kitchen.

Melinda took a deep breath and put the phone to her ear. "Hi, Mom."

"Mindy, sweetheart!" her mother exclaimed. "Don't you know I've been dying to hear from you? Did you fall off the face of the earth over there?"

"I guess I just kept missing your calls," Melinda answered.

"Oh well, never mind. I've been busy, too. It's just that I needed to at least hear your voice. I *miss* you. Sharon tells me things are going fine."

"They are."

"She said you were out shopping with your aunt. Did you need to buy more clothes already?"

"Not clothes. Groceries."

"Groceries?"

"For Aunt Rita's animals."

She chuckled. "Sounds like you're fitting right into the routine of things, shopping for the animals with Rita. Have you signed up for any summer classes or workshops or anything like that yet?"

"Mom, I just got here."

"Oh, that's right, never mind. It feels like you've been gone for weeks already. So did you bring the right clothes?"

"Yes." Today she was wearing the same khaki shorts with a different T-shirt.

"Well, if you need anything we didn't pack, feel free to do a little shopping. And let me know if you need more money."

"I have enough," Melinda said. "Daddy gave me some, too."

Her mother's voice changed. "You've heard from your father already?"

"No, I mean he gave me some before he left."

"So you haven't heard from him?"

"Not yet."

"Well, you will. And when you do, for heaven's sake, don't start worrying about him. He has no one to blame for the summer but himself. The last thing any of us needs is to—"

"Would you like to talk to Aunt Rita again, Mom?" Melinda interrupted. "She's right out on the front porch. You know the porch here, the one with the *swing*?"

A pause. "I'll talk to her another time, Mindy, I called to talk to you."

"I'm fine, Mom. Really. Nothing's happened yet, so I don't have anything to tell you."

Another pause. "Well, you have a great day, sweetheart. But call me after the weekend, okay? I want to hear from you every week."

"I'll try, Mom. But sometimes it's hard to get the phone. Sharon has a new boyfriend and they talk on the phone all the time."

"Try extra hard," her mother insisted. "I love you, darling. I miss you like crazy."

"Love you, too. Good-bye." She hung up, turned around, and there was Sharon in her bathrobe and slippers, her head wrapped in a towel.

"Why did you tell her that part about the phone?" Sharon asked. "You know I have my own phone."

"Otherwise she'll expect me to call her all the time."

Sharon nodded knowingly. "Got the picture. My mom would be the same way." Her smile widened. "You haven't told me yet what you thought of Evan."

Just then Aunt Rita poked her head into the kitchen. "Have a nice talk, Melinda?"

Melinda nodded.

"Well, excuse me for interrupting, but I need Sharon to run to the store for me."

"Mother!" Sharon complained. "Look at me! I'm not even awake yet!"

"This will take you five minutes."

"Mother!"

"I can go," Melinda offered. "I'm all dressed and everything. I'd like to, really."

Aunt Rita scowled at Sharon, but gave Melinda the list. Sharon said sweetly, "When you come back, I promise to be a fully functioning human."

Aunt Rita grumbled, "Let's not make promises we can't keep."

She was coming back from the store, emerging from the tunnel at a half-run, when she nearly collided with Paul, standing at the entrance. She jerked backward just in time, but he had to grab her arms to keep her from falling over. She pushed him away, annoyed. "What are you doing just *standing* there?"

"I'm not just *standing* here. I was waiting for you."

"You nearly caused an accident. What do you want?"

"I wanted to ask you something."

"Well, *what?*"

He stalled. "I was just wondering. I was thinking about our conversation yesterday. I was hoping . . . I've been meaning to ask you—"

"I didn't say anything to her," Melinda said abruptly.

"You didn't say anything?" he repeated. "To Sharon?"

"I just told you, I didn't."

"About what you said about me being hung up on her and what I said about her not caring? You guys didn't talk about it?"

"No, we didn't *talk* about it."

Paul exhaled, relieved. "Well, would you mind not saying anything about it? Like today either?"

He looked so anxious that she said, more kindly, "If you don't want me to, I won't."

A pause. Then he asked, "So you think she doesn't know?"

"She knows you're mad at her. She doesn't know *why*."

He shook his head in disgust at this news. "Wouldn't you think she'd put it all together? The way I just happened to get mad at her when she started hanging around with the Con-man? Wouldn't you think she'd use a few brain cells?"

"She's pretty preoccupied lately," Melinda said. "She hasn't spent more than ten minutes with me and she's really down on her parents."

"Those two? They're the greatest! Man, she has completely lost her mind. What a bimbo."

"Don't call her that," Melinda said protectively. "We're very close. Almost like sisters."

Paul's expression changed. He asked dryly, "And what would you know about sisters?"

"Not very much," Melinda admitted.

"Well, I do. Consider yourself lucky you don't have one like mine. And having Sharon for a sister wouldn't be much of an improvement."

"You're just mad because she's in love with somebody and it's not you," Melinda scolded.

Paul drew back, but insisted quietly, "That's not why."

"Then why?"

He hesitated. "Why should I spill my guts to you?" he asked. "I know how girls are; they tell each other everything."

"I'm a child of divorce, remember?" Melinda said. "I'm used to keeping secrets."

He looked at her intently, deciding whether he could trust her. Then he challenged, "First tell me a comparable secret about yourself."

"Okay," Melinda agreed. She thought a moment. "I'm sick of always being caught between my parents. And I'm sick of worrying about them. I hate it and I'm sick of it and they don't know."

He thought it over, his expression skeptical.

"Hey, it's a real secret!" Melinda said. "If your parents were divorced you'd understand."

"Okay, okay, I accept."

"Then tell me why you're so mad at my cousin."

He sighed, giving in. "Because. Because she thinks I'm just a dumb neighbor kid. She never even gave me a chance."

They were both silent a moment, digesting the intensity of the information they had exchanged. Finally Paul said sarcastically, "Now that we both know something negative about each other, we can have a more balanced relationship."

"Emotional blackmail. Great," Melinda agreed archly.

Paul smirked and said, "A beautiful way to start a friendship."

SIX

 ✦ ❖ ✦

A week had passed. On Melinda's second Monday in St. Joseph, as on her first, she awoke to a silent house, but this time it was because she'd slept so late. Aunt Rita and Uncle Ted had already left the house; Sharon was still sleeping.

Melinda decided she was tired of wearing the same two T-shirts, the same shorts. She wanted to go shopping, alone, without her mother, in the town of St. Joseph. She walked through the quiet, shady streets downtown, wandering in and out of several clothing shops until she found one she liked and picked out two outfits for herself—simple shirt and shorts combinations in pretty colors, dark rose and lavender. She also bought a cotton jumper, a shapeless but cheery yellow plaid. But as she looked in the dressing room mirror, something about her face bothered her. *It's my hair,* she decided. It hung like dark curtains at either side of her head and pulled her whole face down.

Near the clothing shop was a salon with a sign in the

window: WALK-INS WELCOME. Ten minutes later, she was in a salon chair, watching swatches of shoulder-length hair fall to the floor around her feet. It didn't take long, less than half an hour, but the change was startling. Melinda's new haircut was a thick bob, the sides chin-length, the back shorter. She looked both more sophisticated and more playful. Less serious. It was a real transformation.

Halfway home, she noticed someone leaning over his bicycle on the next block. It was the hair she recognized first, dark and wildly curly all around his face, like untrimmed poodle fur. Paul was dressed completely in white, a tennis racket in a shoulder case across his long, narrow back. When he looked up and saw Melinda, he looked back down at his bike at first, then did a double take, his eyes widening under his thick eyebrows. "What did you do to your hair?" he asked.

"It's a haircut," Melinda said huffily. She asked back, "What did *you* do to your bike?"

He gave the back tire a frustrated kick as she came closer. "I don't know," he grumbled. "My lower gears are totally screwed up—they keep popping in and out when I change speeds. Guess I'd better walk it back and ask Mother dearest if I can drive her car to my tennis lesson." Then he laughed—an abrasive, scoffing laugh—at the very idea.

"She'll say no?" Melinda asked.

He scowled. "First she'll give me a list of reasons why she couldn't possibly say yes. For my own good. Then she'll say no."

His expression became more hopeful. "Hey, you drive, Melinda?"

She shook her head, feeling young. "Next year."

Paul looked surprised. He asked, "You're that much younger than Sharon?"

"I'll be a sophomore."

"I'm a junior. Man, you sure look older than a sophomore," Paul said. "Especially with your hair all chopped off like that."

"My hair is not all *chopped* off. Maybe you should talk someone into chopping off some of *yours*."

Paul made a mock-insulted face, then laughed. Melinda did, too, in spite of herself. They fell into step together, the bike between them, Melinda clutching her packages. When she stole a sideways glance at him, she saw the frustrated look again. "Will you miss your tennis lesson?" she asked.

"Man, I spent over a hundred dollars on this stupid racket," he grumbled. "Why did I even bother? Summer goals are such a waste of time."

"I don't have any goals this summer," Melinda confessed. "It feels so weird. Like I'm just floating around here. Like I'm free."

"Free from what?"

"Free from trying to be who my mother thinks I am when I'm with her and who my father thinks I am when I'm with him. Sometimes I start to feel like I'm two people in one body. But since I came here, I'm just . . . me. Melinda."

"The Melinda Zone," Paul said helpfully. They were in front of his house, and he started dragging his bike up the stairs of his porch.

"The Melinda Zone," she repeated behind him. She liked the sound of it.

He added, before he disappeared inside, "I like the hair."

Melinda touched the back of her newly cropped head and smiled.

It was the big news at dinner. "I am so jealous!" Sharon exclaimed. "You have such perfect hair for a bob. Mine has always been too curly."

"I just hope your Mother doesn't have a fit when she sees it," Aunt Rita said worriedly. "I swear, you look five years older."

"Aunt Liz will love it," Sharon insisted. "That cut is totally in style this summer."

"So you two spent the day downtown together?" Uncle Ted asked approvingly.

A pause. Sharon looked at Melinda. Then she said, lifting her chin, "I had other plans."

Uncle Ted's expression changed. "What other plans?"

"I promised to help Evan with some bookkeeping stuff for his band. It took us the whole afternoon."

Uncle Ted looked down at his plate, as if he were counting. When he looked up, he said, "This is the first afternoon you've had off in a week, Sharon. I think it's pretty inconsiderate of you not to spend it with Melinda."

Melinda interjected quickly, "I didn't ask her to come with me, Uncle Ted. I felt like shopping alone."

Uncle Ted looked unconvinced. He turned back to Sharon. "When was the last time you spent a free afternoon with *any* of your friends?"

"Oh, please, not this again," Sharon groaned.

Uncle Ted pointed a finger at her across the table. "If you don't make time for your friends, what kind of a friend does that make you? We haven't all dropped off

he face of the earth, you know, just because you don't
have time for us anymore."

Melinda's stomach twisted into a knot. Aunt Rita
stood up, making calm-down gestures with her hands,
preparing to speak, but Sharon and Uncle Ted ignored
her. Sharon said, "I've explained this a million times,
Pops, if you'd listen! This is a very unusual summer for
me. Evan is leaving as soon as it's over. My *friends* understand that!"

Uncle Ted demanded, "I want to know why you can't
find a little time to spend with—"

"She did," Melinda interrupted breathlessly. She looked
meaningfully at Sharon. "We are. We're spending some
time together tonight."

Sharon didn't miss a beat. "Evan and I are taking her
to the Riverwatch."

"I didn't have anything to wear," Melinda said.
"That's why I went shopping."

A moment of silence. Aunt Rita sat down and patted
Uncle Ted's hand. Sharon raised her eyebrows at Melinda: *A close call.* "Well, it's about time," Uncle Ted
said. "And that's all I'm saying about *that.*"

"Your timing was perfect," Sharon said to Melinda's reflection. They were sitting side by side at Sharon's vanity,
Melinda watching Sharon outline and color her eyelids.
"It's eighteen-and-under night at the Riverwatch. We can
show off your new haircut to all the cute guys."

"Sharon," Melinda asked hesitantly. "Were you actually dating Paul when you met Evan?"

Sharon shrugged. "We might have gone to a few mov-
es together. No big deal."

"For him either?"

She looked less sure. "Well, you know he's a year younger than I am," she said, as if it explained everything. "He's kind of immature."

"Why do you say that?"

"There's something about him—he's got some kind of chip on his shoulder, something about his parents or his sister. I could never figure it out. I mean, his mom and dad are normal. Sort of out of it, but what's new? It's not like they *abuse* him or anything."

She turned from the mirror to look at Melinda. "Why are you asking me so many questions about Paul?"

"No reason," Melinda insisted. "It's just that I see him sitting on his porch all the time."

"I know. He's wasting the summer away, sitting on his throne over there. Some people have no motivation, Mindy. I don't have time for it. Especially not this summer." She added meaningfully, "This summer is for Evan."

Evan didn't hide his surprise when both Sharon and Melinda climbed into his van.

"We owe Melinda a favor," Sharon explained. "She saved me from getting the third degree from my dad again."

But when they told him about the Riverwatch, he complained, "Aw, Sharon, it's kid night over there tonight. Nobody else will be there. You guys sure you wouldn't rather just go to a movie?"

"I want Melinda to see where we met," Sharon insisted. "Come on, Evan, we'll just go for a little while.

Melinda needs to be entertained. My parents are driving her up the wall."

She smiled at Melinda in the backseat of the van, a grateful, conspiratorial smile, then asked Evan, "What do you think of her new haircut?"

"Whose new haircut?"

"Evan! My cousin's new haircut!"

He looked over his shoulder at Melinda. "Hey, nice," he said. Then he grinned at Sharon, teasing her. "She looks older than you now, kid."

"She does not," Sharon pouted. "And stop calling me kid." But she hung on his arm as they walked in, Melinda walking slightly behind them. She felt strange being with them, stranger still once they were inside. The crowd was young and noisy and to them, Evan O'Connor was obviously something of a celebrity. People were whispering behind their hands and pointing to them as they found an empty table near the stage. Half a dozen girls walked by, calling out hellos to him, their voices shrill over the din of the canned music. Sharon clung tightly to his arm, smiling either up at him, or past him, at Melinda, asking her with her eyes, *See how lucky we are, to be with someone like him?*

But when the canned music stopped and the band came out on the stage, Evan's expression changed. He sat forward in his chair and pointed to the band. "Son of a bitch!" he exclaimed. "What the hell is Dave doing up here?"

Sharon followed his gaze and then pointed and explained anxiously to Melinda, "Uh-oh. It's Dave, the drummer for the Con-Artists."

Evan got up and left them, barreling up to the stage before the band started its set. He argued for a few minutes with his drummer, then came back to the table scowling and cursing under his breath. "I can't believe he would agree to play with these morons. It makes us all look bad. Jesus, Dave is such an idiot."

When the music started, he grew even angrier, throwing up his hands, complaining after every song. "These guys are pathetic. Maybe I should fire Dave, see how he likes being with them permanently."

"Come on, Evan," Sharon pleaded. "He was just trying to help out another band. Besides, it's eighteen night, it isn't important."

But Evan ignored her, sulking and tossing back his head, glaring at the musicians, his arms crossed. Melinda could tell that Sharon was embarrassed; she had let go of his arm and was fidgeting on the table with her fingertips. Melinda struggled to think of a way to get out of the situation. After half an hour, Evan's mood worsening with every song, she leaned close and whispered to Sharon, "I need to go home. I don't feel well, I think I might be getting my period."

"We need to leave," Sharon announced to Evan after the next song. "We've both had enough of your temper." She took Melinda's hand and stormed from the club.

"You can just drop me off at the house," Melinda said as they climbed into the van.

Evan followed close behind. "Hey, what is your problem?" he asked Sharon, climbing behind the wheel. "This has nothing to do with you, Sharon, this is a professional thing."

"And you were acting so professional," Sharon snapped

They squabbled all during the drive back to the house. Melinda thought they would drop her off and leave to continue their argument, but Sharon got out of the van with her.

"Thank you for a really crummy evening," she told Evan from between her teeth.

"Hey, wait a minute—will you just listen to me?" He followed her onto the porch, defending himself. Melinda hurried up to her room, relieved to be away from them. Below her window, she could hear them still arguing on the front porch—Sharon's voice accusing and wavering, Evan explaining and cajoling, sometimes barking at Sharon in his own defense. Melinda wondered if her aunt and uncle were in their bedroom; she worried that they would overhear. She wondered if Paul could hear from across the street. *Just leave,* she told Sharon and Evan silently. *Go somewhere else and leave us all in peace.*

"Is that one of the blouses you bought yesterday?" Aunt Rita asked her at the breakfast table.

Melinda nodded. "Everything my mom bought me for the summer is too fancy. I needed some things that were more casual."

"I love that shade of purple," Aunt Rita said. "But I can't get used to the haircut. It's like you grew up too fast."

Melinda insisted, "It's me."

"I know it's you. Did you know your Grandma Tremblay used to wear her hair in a bob. I've never noticed before how much you look like her. So did you have a good time at the Riverwatch? You were in your room when Ted and I came back from our walk and I didn't get to ask you."

"I felt a little strange, being there with Evan," Melinda admitted. "Everybody seems to know him."

Aunt Rita acted as if this didn't surprise her. "We can't help worrying about Sharon, being with someone who has such a . . . following. She doesn't call any of her girlfriends from school anymore. That's what Ted was trying to get across to her last night. And it really bothers us that you're spending so much time alone here. You could sign up for some summer programs, you know— the Y offers all kinds of things for teenagers."

Melinda shook her head. "I don't mind just being here alone."

"You don't, do you? Your mother was the same way, you know. Always wanting her privacy. Sometimes I would ask her what she was doing up in her room and she would say, 'Planning a future, somewhere else.' "

"Aunt Rita," Melinda insisted softly, "I'm not like my mom. My mom wants me to be doing something every minute. But I need to just do nothing. I've never in my life felt like I could just do nothing and it would be okay."

Aunt Rita was surprised. She thought for a moment, then agreed slowly. "No . . . no, I don't suppose doing nothing would suit either one of them."

"I don't care if it suits them. It's my summer and this is what I need—to do nothing here."

"But what do you think about, honey, alone in your room so much?"

"I remember things. I think about things. I think about how different it's been for me than for other kids. Because of the divorce."

Aunt Rita tipped her head in concern. "And does it upset you to think about that, Melinda?"

"Not here," Melinda said. "I don't have to worry about either of them here. About what they want or how they want me to be."

Aunt Rita took one of Melinda's hands and squeezed it. "Your parents both want what's best for you, you know that, don't you?"

"I know, I know. But I also know that I need some time to just be me."

"I want you to have whatever you need here," Aunt Rita said. "You can make those decisions for yourself. If that means doing nothing, so be it. Because you're helping us, too. Can you tell? You're quite a peacemaker, Melinda, even when you're off duty."

"I get a lot of practice," Melinda said ruefully.

"I have to go to work now," Aunt Rita said. She began gathering up her belongings for work—her purse and assorted bags of feed and produce for the animals—but she stopped in the kitchen doorway. "Thank you for confiding in me," she announced softly. "I can't tell you what it means to me. But there is one thing I'd like you to do today. Find a minute to give your mom a call. I know how much I'd be needing to hear from you, if I were her."

Melinda nodded. After Aunt Rita left, she considered calling her mother. Confiding in Aunt Rita had made her miss her. Suddenly, she had a clear picture in her mind of the two of them together, sitting at either end of the white leather sofa, both studying, their legs entangled. Melinda could almost smell her mother's gardenia scent and hear the rustle of her robe. All the rest of the morning, she thought about her mother. But she didn't call her.

• • •

That afternoon, a second letter came from England. *Dear Linda*, she read.

It concerns me that I have not yet heard from you. Every day I search the mail for a letter from you, thinking surely today will be the day I hear something. I don't know how to interpret your silence and I don't know how to respond to it. I have to hope that your summer is going well, without really knowing what these weeks have meant to you. What are you doing? How are you spending your time? As for myself, I've been terribly busy, but I find myself missing you more with each passing day. If there had not been an ocean separating us, I would have come home after the first week of not hearing from you . . .

Melinda put her head back and looked at the porch ceiling. She heard someone clearing his throat. Paul was standing on the sidewalk in front of the house. He pointed to the letter. "I see you're bummed out again."

Melinda put her head back again. "It's the most awful letter," she admitted softly. "It's really depressing."

"Is he having too much fun without you?" Paul asked, puzzled.

"No, it isn't that at all. It's that he . . . misses me too much. He's missed me too much since I was born. Even though I've seen him every weekend of every week of my entire life for fifteen years. I don't think he's ever really accepted the fact that I don't live with him. Although I only did for a year and I don't even remember it."

"Sounds intense," Paul said. "Why d'you think he's like that?"

"Maybe because his own parents died in a car accident when he was young. And then the thing with my mom didn't work out. Sometimes I think he's afraid of losing me, too."

Paul shook his head. "Chill out," he advised, as if Melinda's father were there.

"I try to get him to chill out. I try to make him feel like he won't lose me. But I end up having to always act like everything is fine, everything is wonderful. Even sometimes when it *isn't*."

Her voice had risen, and Paul cringed at its volume and shushed her with his hands. "Look, I don't mean to cut you off, but I don't want to be standing out here like a jerk when Sharon comes out."

"She's still asleep. She sleeps in till noon sometimes."

Paul scowled. "Partying too hard with the Con-man?"

"I don't know, Paul. Don't expect me to start spying on her, okay?"

"I never said you should spy on her. It's just that . . . I can't stand that phony creep. Look, could we take a walk or something? It makes me too nervous to stand around out here."

They walked in silence for the first block. Melinda glanced at Paul sideways, at his profile. He had a surprisingly handsome profile—a wide forehead and a jaw well defined from all the sulking. She broke the silence and asked him, "Why did you call Evan a phony creep?"

He snorted derisively. "She's not his only girlfriend, no matter what she tells you."

Melinda was shocked. "How do you know?"

"Come on, that guy has girls falling all over him night and day."

Melinda insisted, "But you don't have any real proof—"

"Like I need proof. I know his type. And you know what else? Last year Sharon and I used to make fun of couples who go around town with the girl totally worshiping the guy, hanging on his every word. Now she's *doing* it! It makes me sick, it really does." He sighed. "My big goal for the summer is to just forget her."

"You're not succeeding, though, are you?"

His face grew long. "I guess I never met anyone like her before. It was like, for a while there, she totally understood me. I was so happy to think that somebody like her could understand somebody like me."

"I know," Melinda said. "That's the way I felt when I first came here."

Paul looked at her. "Here we go again, Melinda. Spilling our guts." His expression became uncertain.

"Paul, I *won't* tell Sharon," Melinda insisted impatiently. "Why won't you believe me?"

She handed him the letter from England. "Here," she said. "Here's my dad's address in England. If I tell Sharon what you told me, you can write to my dad and tell him . . . tell him . . ."

"Tell him he's completely screwed up your life?" Paul suggested.

Melinda couldn't help laughing. Paul was laughing, too.

"Parents love hearing that," he insisted. "Especially from another continent. What should I tell your mom?"

"Tell her I haven't done one single productive thing since I got here. Not one thing."

"Ah, the do-nothing conspiracy. Guaranteed to make even the best parents question their competency."

Melinda giggled. "Tested by satisfied teens everywhere."

They parted. "Remember to do nothing today!" Paul called.

Melinda called back, "I can do more nothing than you can!"

Sharon was up, sitting at the table, rolling quarters from a coffee can filled with money. Her face was puffy and tired, her hair slicked back from her shower. She gestured for Melinda to sit down with her. "Who were you talking to out there?" she asked.

"Oh . . . Paul."

"Paul?! Across-the-street Paul?"

"I've talked to him a few times. I was out walking this morning and he was walking too."

Sharon gave her a coy, knowing look. "Don't you think he's cute?" she asked. "In a goofy sort of way?"

"I don't think he's cute *or* goofy," Melinda said. She changed the subject. "Where were you last night?"

"Why?" Sharon asked back, suddenly worried. "Are Mom and Pops mad at me?"

"Not that I know of. What happened last night?"

"I didn't get home until three o'clock in the morning!" She giggled behind her hand guiltily. "Oh, Mindy, we were at this fantastic party in Niles—there was a blues band from South Bend and everybody was dancing and it just kept getting better and better and I completely lost track of the time. It was about the most fun I've ever had."

Melinda shrugged. "Maybe they didn't hear you come in."

"Come on!" Sharon scoffed. "My parents not hear me come in? That'll be the day!"

"No, really. We all went to bed kind of early after the movie."

"You guys rented another movie?"

"We went out. To Cinema Six. We saw that new comedy-detective movie. It was really funny, we all liked it."

Sharon shook her head, bewildered. "You really don't mind doing stuff with them, do you?"

Melinda shook her head. "I like it."

"Hmmm, maybe they didn't hear me come in after all. I sure am glad you're around, Cousin." She stretched her arms high over her head, relieved.

"You know, Sharon," Melinda said, "I was just thinking. It might be nice sometime if you would come with us to the movies. It might make your mom and dad accept Evan better."

Sharon looked at her in bewilderment. "I'm with them all the time. I see them every day. What difference would going to a movie make?"

Melinda shrugged, but insisted gently. "I just think it would help."

"Look, it is not my fault that they can't accept what's happening between me and Evan," she said. "I'm not going to pretend that it isn't important, just to make them feel better."

"That's not what I meant," Melinda said.

But Sharon was looking off over her head now, speaking more to herself. "I don't even know who I was before I met Evan. I can only be me when I'm with him. I feel so alive when I'm with him. Everything is real and important and nothing is boring and it just keeps getting stronger and . . ."

Melinda had stopped listening. *Sharon is lost,* she thought. *Lost in the Evan Zone.* She felt both worried for her and disappointed in her.

"Where would I be without Evan?" Sharon finished dramatically, throwing open her arms.

You could have been here for me, Melinda replied silently. *I needed a sister.* But even as she was thinking it, she knew it didn't really make much sense anymore. Her perception of Sharon had changed too much. She had put all her hopes on Sharon, coming to St. Joseph starving for her help, but now, she had to admit, she was becoming Melinda without her.

SEVEN

◆❖◆

"**P**arents fighting over you," Paul remarked softly. "Now that would be different."

"It's terrible," Melinda said. "You feel so responsible." She covered her face with her hands, upset just thinking about it.

"Hey, come on," Paul said. "Look at the bright side. Don't you have two of everything? Two birthdays and two Christmases and all that?"

Melinda uncovered her face. "Why do you want to know that? So you can tell me how lucky I am?"

They were sitting on Paul's porch, Paul in the easy chair, Melinda sprawled on a plastic beanbag chair that stuck to her arms and legs. It was late morning, an unusually hot day, even for July. They were both slightly on edge from the heat.

"Did I *say* you were lucky?" Paul snapped.

Melinda looked away, then grumbled, "Of course I have two of everything."

"Okay, okay, just trying to get the picture. So you

went back and forth every weekend? Did you ever just, like, refuse to go? Dig in your heels and say 'Sorry, folks, but I don't feel like moving this week?' "

"Oh, God, *never*," Melinda said. "I can't even *imagine* doing that. It would have been too traumatic for my dad."

Paul shook his head. " 'Excuse the inconvenience, Dad,' " he said, speaking for her. " 'But I'm not in the mood for a major car trip today.' "

"Never," Melinda echoed.

"How far apart do they live?"

"About seventy-five miles."

"And you'd go to your dad's every weekend?"

"For as long as I can remember. To tell you the truth, I never minded the drive very much. I would use the time to prepare for the other home. The other me. The worst part was the waiting. Waiting to be taken back. Then it would be like I was in this state of limbo."

"Like you didn't know if you were the M one or the L one?"

"Like I was neither one," Melinda said.

"What was it like to leave? I mean, sometimes I think about leaving, getting the hell out of town for a change. But I can't imagine doing it every *weekend*."

"My mom always handled it okay. She would treat it like the whole thing was my idea. And she would make jokes about it—ask me if I was going to Old Mac-Donald's Farm or if Rebecca was ready to go to Sunnybrook."

"My kind of humor."

"I hated it, Paul. But at least she didn't get depressed.

That's worse. Sunday afternoons at my dad's, waiting for Mom to come and honk her horn—that was the worst time. My dad's face would just start to droop and droop because I was leaving."

"Hey," Paul coached, punching her arm gently. "Lighten up, droopy. He's not here."

She went on, "My stepmom tried to help. She would always arrange some sort of project for the three of us to do on Sundays. We would make bread or pie or something out of clay. But I never finished anything. I was always leaving in the middle of things—it was normal for me. Alicia thinks it's why I have trouble at school."

Paul looked surprised. "*You* have trouble at school?"

"Trouble finishing things," Melinda repeated. "Why, do you?"

Paul smirked. "Not so much trouble finishing things—more like trouble *attempting* things."

"Do you have a lot of friends at school?" she asked him.

"Sure," he said. "I mean, not hundreds, but a few." He went on philosophically, "The way I see it, Melinda, at this age, friends are everything. Guys who want to hang around with you, want to listen to what you have to say. Guys who laugh at your jokes. I would never be able to handle school without my friends, I really wouldn't."

"Where are all your friends this summer?"

He sighed. "Well, my best friend, Rick—he's in Dallas until August. And my other friend, Marv, he's pretty seriously dating this girl from Stevensville. And then there's Tim, but he's really out of it lately." He made a face.

"Drugs. His parents put him in rehab. I can't deal with it. So I'm sort of in friendship limbo. But it fits in perfectly with my summer no-goals conspiracy."

Melinda smiled. "Mine too."

"But things will be back to normal by August when Rick comes back. He's a good guy."

"I've had trouble keeping friends," Melinda confided abruptly.

Paul was surprised. "You seem like a person who'd have lots of friends."

Now Melinda was surprised. "I do?"

"Sure. Why would somebody like you have trouble making friends?"

"I don't know. I think it's something I do to myself. Back home whenever I'd meet someone who I'd like to have for a friend, I'd start right away feeling like my life is too busy and complicated with all the going back and forth and always being in the middle of everything. Then it always seemed like it was easier to just be alone."

"You mean the way you're talking to me now—you don't have a friend back home that you can do that with?"

"Paul, it's so different here. It's the Melinda Zone—I'm one person in one place. I don't have to do the Mindy and Linda thing here. It takes so much *energy*."

"Quit doing it, Melinda."

She threw up her hands at him. "Come on, Paul, I can't just—boom—quit."

"I mean *gradually*. Jeez, why use up all your energy on your *parents,* Melinda? Where will that get you?"

Melinda bit her lip, frustrated. He was oversimplifying

everything. But she asked him, "You really think I seem like a person who'd have lots of friends?"

"Sure, you know. Other weird girls like yourself."

They made twisted faces at each other. Then Paul's voice changed, grew mournful. "I thought Sharon was my friend," he said.

Melinda leaned back in the beanbag chair and looked at the porch ceiling, disappointed that he would bring up Sharon when they were having such a good talk about friendship. She went home soon afterward, needing to sort through all they had talked about. It was a common pattern now, a long afternoon conversation with Paul; afterward going over what they had talked about alone in her room. It was the do-nothing conspiracy and the routine of it held her; she felt safe.

The afternoons were full of Paul, but the evenings she spent with her aunt and uncle. They took walks, had cookouts in the backyard, went to movies. One evening, Uncle Ted suggested they go to a drive-in restaurant; they took their hamburgers to the beach and ate them on a beach blanket, facing the lingering sun.

"We've noticed that you're getting to know our neighbor across the street," Uncle Ted said. "We always liked that Paul. He's such a character."

"He's been in the neighborhood almost as long as we have," Aunt Rita added. "I can remember when he used to roar around on his Big Wheel, driving everybody crazy. He was something of a terror back then."

"Was he?" Melinda asked, surprised.

"Oh, absolutely. He used to thrive on getting into trouble," Aunt Rita agreed. "Remember, Ted? He's settled down quite a bit in the last few years."

Melinda asked them, "Why aren't his parents ever home?"

Aunt Rita thought a moment. "They used to be around more often, before his sister left. Now I think they're both pretty busy, working full-time. His mother's a nurse and Mr. DuVale has some kind of position with the local schools. Some type of administrator."

Uncle Ted added, "They're very private people, the Du-Vales. We've never really gotten to know them."

"Does Paul complain about them never being home?" Aunt Rita asked.

"Not complain," Melinda said. "I don't think he minds. I was just curious myself."

"His sister Frieda was such a beautiful girl," Aunt Rita said. "And apparently brilliant. She's at Columbia now. I don't think it's been easy for Paul, having the perfect sister."

"We saw quite a bit of Paul in the spring," Uncle Ted said. "He used to come over and sit on the porch with Sharon."

"They were always laughing out there together about something. They seemed to really have fun together."

Melinda lowered her face, hiding a pang of jealousy. *Fun,* she thought. *Does Paul have as much fun with me?* She wondered if she should try not to be so serious with him, try to hide what was bothering her. She was certainly experienced at that. But it seemed to her that in order to do that, she would have to step back out of the Melinda Zone. And hadn't Paul already taught her that in the Melinda Zone, there was room enough for friends?

She had turned out her light, preparing to sleep, when she heard the now familiar sound of a telephone argument coming from Sharon's room. "You can't mean it!" Sharon cried. "How can you do this to me?"

What else is new? Melinda thought, putting a pillow over her ears. But then Sharon came to the doorway of her room and knocked softly. "Melinda, are you asleep? I need to talk to you!"

Melinda sat up in her bed. "What's wrong?" she asked.

Sharon came inside, shut the door, and leaned against it. "He's leaving early! By the middle of August he'll be *gone*!" She went on raggedly, "It's the other guys in his band. They want to leave early, they don't want to wait. They told him if he doesn't go with them now, they'll leave without him." She knelt on the floor beside Melinda's bed and put her face into her arms at the hopelessness of it all.

"Oh, Sharon, maybe it's better this way," Melinda said impulsively.

Sharon lifted her face, appalled. "That's the sort of thing my mother would say! How can it possibly be better to have him leave early?"

"I mean because he's leaving anyway. Maybe it would be harder for you if it dragged on through September. It seems like it's making you pretty unhappy."

Sharon sat on the bed beside Melinda and took one of her hands. She said urgently, "No, you've got it backward. He's the *only* thing that makes me happy. Nothing's going to make any sense once he's gone."

Melinda shook her head. "Sharon, come on. You've got your mom and dad and me and your other friends.

And school will start up again in September. You'll be all right."

"You don't understand." She lay on her back at the foot of the bed and spoke to the ceiling. "No one understands. Everyone thinks that once Evan is gone it will be as if this summer never happened."

Hearing Sharon say this jarred Melinda. The idea of the summer and all its significance evaporating, like a dream, was chilling. *As if it never happened.* Everything she had learned, everything she had discovered. She lay back and spoke to the ceiling, too. "We have to find a way to make the summer stay with us. Even when it's over. We have to find a way."

Sharon looked at her, nodding, and repeated through her tears, "We have to find a way. You *do* understand."

EIGHT

✦❖✦

"I've decided to really go all out for you folks," Uncle Ted announced the next morning. It was a rare breakfast—all four of them at the table at once. They all waited for what he would say next— even Sharon gave him a red-rimmed, wary glance.

"I made reservations for us all to go see a play together next Saturday night up at that summer theater in Saugatuck." He leaned back in his chair, smiling, proud of himself.

Oh no, Melinda thought.

"Ted!" Aunt Rita exclaimed. "The Red Barn? I've always wanted to see a play there! What a great idea!"

"What night did you say you were considering?" Sharon asked.

"Saturday," Uncle Ted repeated. "And I'm not considering it, I've already bought the tickets."

"I wish you'd asked me," Sharon said. "Because last night I found out that Evan has to leave early. I'm only going to be able to see him two more weekends before he leaves and I couldn't possibly give up a Saturday night."

Shut up, Sharon, Melinda thought. She looked at Aunt Rita; her excited expression had faded.

Uncle Ted cleared his throat. "Sharon, I still think we should go to this play. We need to do something all together. As a family."

Sharon was eating again, everyone watching her. She looked up and said, "It's just impossible. Really."

"Sharon," Aunt Rita said slowly, "you are going to have to explain to Evan that we are all going to this play, whether he's leaving early or not."

"I am not going to explain *anything* to Evan!"

At this Uncle Ted lost his temper. "For God's sake, Sharon, when are you going to realize that there are other people in this world that you owe a little consideration to besides Evan?"

"Consideration?" Sharon exclaimed. "Oh, right, like I haven't been considering you two my whole life. What about what I need? What about the fact that Evan is leaving?"

"Oh, so *what* if he's leaving!" Aunt Rita exclaimed, losing control. "So what, so what, so what!"

There was a long silence. Sharon stood up. "Don't think I don't know that you've both been against him since day one," she announced. "You've never been fair to him. You've never treated him with any respect. You've never—"

"Now wait just a minute—how about the way you've been treating us?" Uncle Ted shouted. "How about how you've treated your cousin here?" He pointed forcefully at Melinda as he spoke. Melinda pushed herself away from the table, put her head into her hands, and burst into tears.

"Oh God, honey," Aunt Rita exclaimed. "Don't *you* cry!" She turned to Sharon and Uncle Ted, angry herself. "You've upset Melinda," she said. "Stop shouting and leave us alone."

Uncle Ted threw down his napkin and left the room without a word. Sharon put a hand on Melinda's arm. "For Pete's sake, Mindy, nobody's mad at you."

Melinda shook her head, unable to speak, and Aunt Rita said, more gently, "Go away, Sharon. Go and apologize to your father, if you want to help."

Sharon asked, "Why should *I* apologize?" Her voice was suddenly also tearful. She left her mother and Melinda alone and ran upstairs, slamming the door of her bedroom.

"Come on, now," Aunt Rita said, pulling Melinda's hands away from her face. "Take a nice, deep breath. There, there."

"I felt like they were fighting over me," Melinda told her.

"That argument had nothing to do with you, Melinda. It started well before you arrived. I should have known that nothing as nice as that could happen this summer . . ." She broke down herself as she said this.

"Don't cry, Aunt Rita," Melinda begged.

Aunt Rita said through her tears, "It was such a sweet idea, wasn't it? She could have at least pretended. It wouldn't have killed her."

She got a box of Kleenex from the counter and they sat together a moment, wiping their eyes. Aunt Rita studied Melinda's face, trying to figure something out. "Don't you ever argue with your mom or your dad?" she asked.

"I'm the peacemaker, remember?"

"But nobody can keep peace all the time. You must get mad at them sometimes."

"I'm mad at them right now," Melinda confessed. "Because of how they were fighting over me before I came here."

"Is that why you keep forgetting to call your mother?"

Melinda nodded. "And my dad wrote me two letters and I haven't written him back yet. I don't know how to explain *why* I'm mad. It's been building up for so long that I don't know where to begin."

"Don't stop talking to them, Melinda," Aunt Rita insisted. "Don't shut them out. I know how much that will hurt them. Find a way to tell them what you're feeling."

"But they won't *like* what I've been feeling," Melinda confessed.

"Tell them anyway. Tell them the truth. Find a way. Anything is better than closing the door on them."

She put her arms around Melinda and spoke into her hair. "Oh, it's such a waste, when people do that. It's such a damn waste, it can break your heart like nothing else. Don't do it."

"I won't," Melinda said, hugging her back. It came to her then, in a flash, that she could choose. Shut the door. Open the door. *Tell them anyway.*

"We should have just gone to the play without her," Melinda overheard Aunt Rita say bitterly. "Now we'll have to put up with her acting like she's doing us all such a huge favor."

But Sharon didn't act like that. She was too miserable about the fact that Evan was leaving early. And she also seemed to realize that something had changed because of her reaction to the play, something had been lost. In Melinda's room, she asked Melinda nervously, "Why did we all get so bent out of shape over this silly play?"

Melinda was folding laundry into piles on her bed; she turned and looked at Sharon accusingly.

"What?" Sharon asked. "Why are you looking at me like that? For Pete's sake, what is the big *deal* about this play?"

"It isn't just the play," Melinda said. "They were trying to arrange a moment. A happy family moment to remember forever."

Sharon looked puzzled and Melinda pointed to the picture on the nightstand beside her bed—the one of herself with her parents.

"Like in that picture," she explained. "There are these moments. They can make up for a lot of other disappointments. The kind of moments where everyone is together and everyone is trying. The play could have been like that."

Sharon looked uneasy. "Well, I'm going, aren't I?" she asked.

Melinda sighed. "You really don't get it, do you? It's too late. Sure, we'll all go, but it's too late to have a family moment."

"You are making zero sense, you know that?" Sharon complained.

The day of the play, Sharon seemed unusually contrite. She hung around her mother, who was home from the store to catch up on the bookkeeping. Sharon sat at the table with her, trying to initiate conversation, asking questions about the animals, what her mother was planning to wear to the play. But Aunt Rita held back, preoccupied, looking up from time to time from her books, answering in monosyllables. "Go and talk to your father," she told Sharon, but Uncle Ted was in the garden with earphones on.

On the hour-long drive to the playhouse, they were all silent, lost in separate thoughts. On the walk from the parking lot to the theater Sharon took both her mother's and her father's hands and held them, Melinda thought, a little wistfully. Melinda held back a bit, watching them; they were walking slowly, as if they were all very tired. They walked into the theater that way. It was a kind of good-bye to themselves, to the lost moment. They all sensed it.

That night, Melinda had a dream. She was in a theater, part of an audience, watching a play, a play about the Parker family. Then she was in the play, up on the stage, surrounded by a cast of relatives, all angry. Then the stage changed, became the living room of her father's farmhouse. But Melinda didn't want to be there; she didn't want to miss the end of the play; it seemed terribly important not to miss it. She hurried from the house and into the woods behind the property to find her way back to the theater. But through the trees, she heard an awful sound behind her, a huge roaring wind, like a cyclone, and when she turned around to look back, she saw the farmhouse, with the shadow of her father at the window, engulfed in flames.

NINE
• ❖ •

Finally, after five rings, her mother answered. At the
sound of her familiar voice, Melinda said simply,
"It's me."

Her mother cried, "Mindy, darling!"

"Did I call too early?" Melinda asked.

"No, never, sweetheart, I was already awake. I've been
awake for hours, I'm studying for my last exam. I'm so
glad you called—I've been missing you so much!"

Melinda answered, her voice catching in her throat,
"Me too."

"It's so wonderful to hear your voice! Why haven't you
called—it's been over two weeks without a single word!"

"I know. I'm sorry, I've been kind of busy." She scram-
bled for an explanation. "I went shopping," she said
lamely. "And I got my hair cut. Kind of short. And I
made a new friend here. A boy."

She added silently, *And I had a terrible dream about
Daddy.*

"That doesn't sound so awfully busy. What classes are you taking?"

"I decided that I want to be called Melinda from now on."

After a long pause her mother asked, "What's going on over there? Do you want to come home now?"

The question took Melinda by surprise. "Come home?" she repeated.

"Honey, if you're bored, I can have you on the train tomorrow."

"Mom," Melinda said in a more careful voice. "Mom, it's probably better if I just stay here. Until you're done with your workshop."

But her mother insisted, "My workshop is almost over. There isn't any real need for you to be away now, honestly."

"I want to stay," Melinda insisted. She held her breath.

Her mother was silent. Finally she said, "You sound so different, Mindy."

"Melinda."

Another silence. Then her mother spoke again. "Well, *Melinda*. I guess you're saying I should finish up my business here, like we planned, is that it?"

"Yes."

"And then I'll drive up to get you in early August, okay? What would be a good day?"

Melinda looked at the calendar. "The fifteenth?"

Her mother repeated, "The fifteenth? You're sure?" A sigh. "All right, my wandering girl. I'm proud of you for being so independent. But won't you get a few French workbooks from the library and at least keep up with your French?"

"*Au revoir*, Mom," Melinda answered.

"She asked me to come back," Melinda told Paul. "She said she could have me on the train tomorrow."

"Did she freak out when you said no?"

"My mom never freaks out, Paul," Melinda explained. "She isn't the type. She's on top of everything. Anyway, that isn't why I called her. I just wanted to talk to her."

"About what?"

"I had this dream last night. I guess it made me miss her."

Paul looked curious. "A bad dream? A nightmare?"

Melinda nodded.

"And you would actually tell your mom about a nightmare?"

Melinda asked back, "Wouldn't you tell your mom about a nightmare?"

He laughed out loud at this. "Oh, *sure*! Especially all the ones I have about her!"

Before Melinda could respond, he said abruptly, "So tell *me* about your nightmare."

Then he grinned at her, the challenging, can-you-handle-it grin. Melinda didn't like seeing it. Paul picked up a magazine from the floor beside his lounger and pretended to be writing furiously on it. "So vat vas da nature of dis veird dream?"

"This isn't funny, Paul," Melinda said darkly.

"Hey, I'm just kidding."

"You're always kidding, aren't you? You think everything is a big dumb joke, don't you?"

He looked shocked at her vehemence. "Hey, what are you getting mad at me for?"

She stood up. "I don't *like* it when people make jokes about things that aren't *funny*."

"Okay, okay, sorry. Really. So it's not funny, so sit down and relax."

"I don't want to sit down," she griped. "You've got me all hyped up, I feel really nervous now. Look, can we go somewhere? Can we take a walk somewhere? I need to walk."

"Fine, let's go. It's almost lunchtime, we can get hot dogs and eat them on the bluff."

"I couldn't eat a hot dog if my life depended on it," Melinda complained. She clutched at her waist as they walked.

"O-*kay*, forget hot dogs," Paul said. "We'll just head downtown and maybe you'll get hungry on the way. Maybe you'll relax a little, okay?"

He seemed sorry to have upset her. He kept nudging her arm to snap her out of it. After a block of silence, Melinda confessed quietly, "I couldn't have told my mom the dream, Paul. She would have made a joke about it. She would have said something like, 'It's about time somebody burned that place down.' I can just hear her."

"You burned something down in your dream?" Paul asked curiously.

Melinda bit her lip and looked away.

"Come on," Paul urged. "You can tell me."

"Don't pressure me!" Melinda snapped. "You are *always* pressuring me to tell you things."

"I am not!" Paul said, losing patience. "Come off it, Melinda—you think you're the only person in the world who has nightmares?"

"No, I *don't* think that. But knowing you, you'll probably just say 'Big deal—you call that a nightmare?' Or 'Why don't you just *quit* having nightmares?' "

Now Paul was exasperated. "I've *had* nightmares, Melinda. I won't argue with you about whether or not it was really a *nightmare*."

"You argue with me about everything *else*!" Melinda cried.

They glared at each other and then both broke into nervous giggles. Paul said, "We do argue a lot, don't we?"

"I think I'm making up for lost time," Melinda replied.

"Not me," Paul said. "I argue with everybody. It keeps my mind alert. I argue with animals. I argue with plants. I argue with inanimate objects."

"Do you ever argue with your parents?"

He corrected himself. "*That* is a waste of energy. My motto is: Never be in the same room with parents long enough to argue with them."

"How about friends? Do you argue with friends?"

"Sure, once in a while. You can't agree all the time." He pointed out, "You and I argue and we're friends."

She was both touched to hear him say that and a little disappointed. She looked at him sideways; he was squinting, pointing across the street at a hot dog stand, a cart with an awning and a hand-painted sign. "There it is—my favorite dining establishment. Sure you don't want a hot dog? My treat."

Melinda grimaced. "My stomach is in a knot."

He rolled his eyes. "Are you always this much fun to take to lunch?"

He bought two hot dogs and carried them in a cardboard boat to a picnic table on the bluff. They sat down together, both facing the lake. Paul ate both hot dogs in three bites apiece. When he saw that Melinda was gazing toward the shimmering lake, he said, "We should go to the beach sometime."

Melinda hesitated. "I'm not much of a beach person," she told him. Actually she couldn't imagine being with Paul while she was wearing a bathing suit. She was sure he would say something rude about how tall and thin she was.

"Me either," Paul said. "I prefer not to appear too often in public in a bathing suit. It's too hard on all the girls."

"What a compassionate guy," Melinda said.

They began walking again. As they walked, Melinda began to speak. She recited softly, as if talking to herself, "In the dream I was standing in the woods near my dad's house, and I heard this noise. This awful, whooshing noise, like a train, but more scary. Then when I looked back at my dad's house, it was all on fire. And I couldn't do anything about it. I just watched it burn."

Paul was silent a moment. Then he finally said, in a tone of recognition, "That's a dream about being scared to get mad."

She stopped walking in surprise. "How do *you* know?"

"It means you're afraid your anger will be too destructive and wreck everything. If you let it out."

Melinda considered this explanation. "It does make sense, in a way. I am afraid to tell them I'm angry. I've actually been avoiding talking to them. Do you think I'm afraid that my anger will wreck my father's farm?"

"Not the actual farm, Melinda. Just the way things were before."

She nodded to herself, thinking. Then she looked at

Paul, her eyes wide with appreciation. "Sometimes you amaze me. You are really so smart about this stuff."

"Don't mention it. How's your stomach?"

"It's better," she admitted, surprised. "I think I could even eat something now!"

But they had walked several blocks away from downtown. "How about if I make you a sandwich at my house?" Paul suggested. "Can your sensitive stomach tolerate peanut butter?"

It was the first time he had offered to take her inside his house. Melinda felt a little crunch of excitement, as if they were crossing an important boundary. But once they were on his porch, he seemed more wary. "Brace yourself," he told her. "You are about to enter the Country Living National Museum."

He was right. Both the living room and the dining room were decorated in layers of calico and gingham with tiered curtains and dried-flower wall hangings and shiny wood floors and baskets everywhere. The kitchen was all in blue, gingham and delft and stenciled ducks with blue ribbons around their necks—an incongruous setting for Paul. He opened his refrigerator and pulled out a jar of peanut butter. "I warned you," he said.

"It's very cozy," Melinda said politely.

He made a rude sound.

"Where is your room?" she asked, and he pointed to a hallway off the kitchen. "Through there. First door on the right. Go ahead and take a look if you want to." He shrugged, as if it didn't matter. Melinda went through a small hallway with a bathroom on one side and a closed door on the other. She opened the door and peeked in.

Paul's room was completely different from the rest of the house—it was very plain and spare, surprisingly tidy; nothing out of place on the floor or the dresser top, the bed made without a crease. At first it was this tidiness that caught her off guard; it wasn't what she would have expected from Paul, with his rumpled clothes and crazy hair. It wasn't until she shut the door that it hit her— the way everything was beige and bare and uninhabited-looking. Paul came up behind her while she was looking. "What's the matter?" he asked. "Don't you like my room?"

She took a step away and accidentally pressed into him, his chest and shoulders against her back. He didn't move. She could smell the peculiar mix of shampoo and soap and deodorant that was his smell. They leaned together for a moment. "Don't you like my room?" he asked again.

Melinda smiled at him over one shoulder. She said sarcastically, breaking the spell, "It's very tasteful."

Adding to herself, as they walked away, *Safe. Like mine.*

The final month of summer found Paul and Melinda content with the empty days. Their conversations began on the neutral territory of their respective porches and took them through the quiet streets of the neighborhood, or along the bluff. Melinda noticed that, except for an occasional cryptic one-liner, Paul never talked about his own family, but in many ways it suited her to be the talker, the one who was defining her situation and her relationships. Paul listened and responded in a way that also suited her—both curious and detached, both reassuring and blunt. And he could make her laugh, even when she was remembering something difficult, something that made her angry.

"Talking to you really helps me," Melinda said one afternoon, before she left his porch.

"Yeah, it helps me too," Paul said.

Melinda thought he was referring to his own family and didn't understand how he was being helped, but then he qualified, "Helping me get over Sharon, I mean."

"Oh." Melinda looked away.

"Want to get an ice cream bar at Mickey's before you go home?"

"I'm almost out of money," Melinda protested. "We have ice cream. My aunt won't mind if you have some."

But when they got to the Parkers' front porch, Paul hung back and said, "I'll just wait out here."

He would never come inside the Parker house. He even acted a little panicky at the thought; he would get a trapped look in his eyes. It always made her feel a pang of disappointment in him. Sometimes she imagined herself dragging him inside by the arm, right up to Sharon's bedroom, demystifying Sharon so that Paul would finally just get over her. *We're running out of time,* she wanted to shout at him.

TEN

❖

The telephone rang while Melinda was eating breakfast alone. Paul had promised to call; they had talked about a bike ride. But instead of Paul's voice, she heard background static. "Linda? Linda, it's Daddy."

"Daddy!" Melinda exclaimed. She felt something lurch inside her, at her heart. "Daddy, are you all right?"

"I guess I'm all right. Linda, please explain to me why I haven't heard one word from you since I left in June."

Melinda was suddenly terribly sorry. "Oh, Daddy, it's been impossible to write. I honestly tried to, but I just . . . I didn't know how to explain what's been happening with me here."

"Linda, I want to understand. What *is* happening to you there?"

Melinda tried to find the words; she stammered apologetically for a few minutes. Then she took a deep breath and said, "Well, for one thing, I've changed my name to Melinda."

There was a crackling silence. When her father spoke, it was in a rush. "I want you to listen to me a moment, Linda. There's something I want you to do. Alicia left England yesterday. I've decided it would be a good idea for you to spend the rest of the summer on the farm with her, helping her with the orchard. If you're uncomfortable explaining to your relatives why you're leaving early, Alicia can talk to them. I know it isn't the way we planned it, but I think it would be better for you to be home. I'm worried about you. I think I was pressured into a decision that wasn't best for you."

"But, Daddy, I'm not ready to come home yet."

"Why not? Are you in the middle of classes?"

"Not classes, but . . ."

"Then there shouldn't be any problem. I want you with Alicia. It's been too difficult, being out of touch with you. I won't ever do this again. Alicia should be settled in by tomorrow. She'll call you sometime in the evening. I'll be joining the two of you in just a few short weeks, so please don't make any other plans before Labor Day. All right, Linda? All right?"

Melinda felt as though the static from the phone had entered her brain. She managed to say, "But I had some things I wanted to tell you."

"We'll have plenty of time to talk. I have things to tell you, too. I can't tell you how much I've missed you. Expect to hear from Alicia tomorrow night. All right? All right now, Linda? We'll straighten this all out, and we'll have plenty of time to talk, I promise, all right?"

He said good-bye. Then she heard a click and an empty buzz, proof that an ocean was between them again.

Sharon had come into the kitchen from her shower, a

towel over her head. She groaned, "Was that the Riverwatch calling again?"

"It was my dad," Melinda said tonelessly. "Calling from London. He wants me to spend the rest of the summer on the farm with Alicia."

Sharon's face fell. She sat down beside Melinda and said urgently, "But you told him no, right?"

"I didn't know what to say. I wasn't prepared."

"You can't leave now, Melinda. My mom and dad really need you."

Melinda drew back at this, offended. She said, "Don't tell me that. I don't need to hear that."

Sharon's eyes widened in surprise. She said innocently, "But, Melinda, I only meant ... I mean, you've been saying all along that you didn't mind doing things with them."

"I don't mind. But don't try to make me feel like now I can't leave. They're *your* parents, Sharon."

"Well, I know *that*," Sharon said. "I just don't want you to go. You have to at least stay until my birthday! Can't you make up an excuse or something? I know— tell your mom and dad you've met a guy you can't live without, that'll flip them out. Tell them you can't leave Paul." She giggled, expecting Melinda to laugh with her.

But Melinda didn't laugh.

"Uh-oh," Sharon teased. "Mindy looks pretty serious. What's going on with you and Paul?"

"My name is Melinda. And Paul is just a neighbor, remember?"

"Not to you," Sharon said. "Maybe to you he's an incredibly exotic and exciting boy from another town." She giggled again.

"Well, he doesn't have a following of girls at the Riverwatch," Melinda retorted. "If that's what you consider exotic."

She left Sharon, open-mouthed, at the kitchen table and left the house to find Paul.

Paul listened to her description of her father's phone call, trying to recover his breath. They had cycled nearly five miles together and were resting at a sparse roadside park with a solitary table and grill and a wide view of Lake Michigan, glass-like today, the water silver in the August haze.

"What *is* it with your dad?" Paul asked abruptly. "How can he expect you to just drop everything and rush back to Wisconsin now?"

"He's worried that I've changed."

"So *what* if you've changed? Everybody changes all the time. Maybe *he* should change."

"Maybe you should change. Maybe we should all change. Maybe it's just not that *simple*, okay?"

Paul backed off. "All right, all right," he said. "Fill me in some more about this stepmother person. All you've said about her is that she runs the farm and organizes Sunday-afternoon projects."

"She's just . . . Alicia. She's been with my father for as long as I can remember."

"So you're pretty used to her?"

"I don't want to spend the rest of the summer with her, but yes, I'm used to her."

"But you're not that close to her, right? You don't, like, *love* her." Paul cringed as he said this.

Melinda thought about it. Alicia's face came into her

mind, her expression distracted—the way she often looked when she came in from the pottery studio or the apple orchard. Alicia didn't seem to really need anything from her, nothing but basic courtesy. Melinda tried for a moment to imagine what it would have been like if Alicia had wanted the same intense loyalty that her parents expected. She was grateful that she didn't. But, answering Paul's question, Melinda said, "No, I guess I don't really love her."

"She probably doesn't love you, either," Paul said logically. "Tell her to tell your dad you're not coming home early. It will be good practice for when you have to say no to *him*."

"You're right," Melinda agreed. "It will."

"That'll be seventy-five dollars, please."

Melinda laughed. "I probably owe you about a million by now!"

"Yeah, yeah," he said, shrugging.

"How do you know so much about things like this, Paul?" Melinda asked.

But he had gotten back onto his bike and was coasting ahead. "Come on," he called. "Let's get back. I bought a new reggae tape yesterday and we can listen to it on my porch."

"No way," Melinda protested. "I'm boycotting reggae for the rest of the summer. Play it when I'm not around."

Paul pushed off on his bike, saying over one shoulder, "You need to work a little harder on being able to say no."

She was sitting between her aunt and uncle, watching television, when the phone rang. Her aunt made a move to shift the cat from her lap to Uncle Ted's, but Melinda stood up. "I'll get it," she said. "I think it might be for me."

It was. "Hey, girl," Alicia said, her voice relieved. "How *are* you?"

"I'm fine, Alicia. Are you home?"

"Yes and thank heavens. I can't tell you how good it feels to be back out in the country again, away from smog and traffic and tourists."

"Are the animals okay?"

"Everyone survived. My girls aren't laying yet, they're sulking in the henhouse, but everything should be back to normal in a few more days. What about you? We were worried about you, Linda. Why didn't you ever write to us?"

"I don't know," Melinda said. "It's hard to explain."

"Did your dad get ahold of you?"

"I talked to him yesterday."

"So you know about him wanting you to come to the farm? Have you decided if you want me to drive up there and pick you up? Or would you rather take the train?"

"Alicia . . . I think I'd rather stay here until Daddy comes back. I don't really want to leave early."

Alicia was silent a moment, digesting this news. When she spoke, she didn't sound hurt, or even surprised, but her voice was uncertain. "Linda, I'll have to tell your father and he'll think something is wrong."

Melinda said, "Something *is* wrong."

"Something is wrong?" Alicia repeated. "Do you want to tell me what?" When Melinda hesitated, she added, more insistently, "Are you all right, Linda?"

"It's more like . . . something *was* wrong," Melinda

explained haltingly. "I was ... I was ... upset when I first came here. About my mom and dad fighting. I've had a lot of time to think about it, but I still need a little more time. I want to be able to tell them some things. About me."

"Oh, Linda," Alicia said. Her voice was anxious, too. "This sounds so intense. What will I tell your father? I don't want him to worry. He's all by himself now over there."

"Alicia, I worry about *him* all the time. So let him worry about me for a change."

Alicia exclaimed softly in surprise. But when she spoke again, her voice was different. "All right, Linda," she said. "Here's what I'll do. I'll call your dad and tell him that you've decided to stay right where you are until he gets back. I won't tell him anything else. And in the meantime let's make a deal. Let's promise we'll *both* stop worrying about your dad. What do you say?"

"I promise, if you promise," Melinda said.

"I promise."

After she hung up, she wondered why it had been so easy. Then it hit her—something that had been missing from Paul's advice. *It's because I'm here,* she realized. *I can say no to them here.* She had a sudden, intense desire to have both parents see her in the Melinda Zone. In this place, in this room, in a world separate from either of them. Her heart began to beat faster. Impulsively, she called Alicia back and said, "I want to stay for Sharon's birthday on the fourteenth. Tell Daddy to come and get me on the fifteenth."

"I'm writing it on the calendar," Alicia said. "I'll call your father tomorrow."

Melinda hung up and clapped her hands to her cheeks, shocked at what she had done. She wanted to tell Paul.

It was strange to knock on his front door in the evening; their friendship seemed so firmly relegated to daylight. An older woman answered Melinda's knocking, heavyset and dark-haired with an old-fashioned bouffant hairdo, peppered with gray. "I'm Paul's friend from across the street," Melinda explained. "Melinda Morrison. I was just wondering if he's home."

"I'm Mrs. DuVale," the woman said. "Nice to meet you, dear." Her voice was pleasant, but formal. "Paul is in his room."

She gestured for Melinda to follow her. Paul was lying on his perfectly made bed, wearing earphones, jiggling one leg. Melinda could faintly hear the Jamaican music he was listening to. When he saw Melinda behind his mother, he took off his earphones, but didn't get up. His mother asked quietly, "Could you take your feet off the bed, Paul?"

"No, I couldn't take my feet off the bed, Mom."

"Then could you please take off your dirty shoes?"

"My shoes aren't dirty," he said. He held up his feet so that she could see the bottoms. "Are they, Mom?"

His mother sighed and left the room. Paul got up and closed the door of his bedroom. He caught Melinda's accusing look and insisted, "She started it. What's up? You look pretty wired tonight."

"I just told my stepmom that I wasn't coming back early."

"Way to go," Paul congratulated her. He gestured for

her to sit in the beige canvas director's chair at the foot of his bed.

Melinda leaned forward excitedly. "Paul, I got this idea after I talked to my stepmom. I wanted to tell you. I'm going to arrange it so that both my parents come here at the same time."

"Together?"

She nodded. "And they won't know what's going on until they get here."

Paul's eyebrows rose. "Intense," he pronounced. "But, Melinda, I thought you generally try to avoid getting them together."

"The point isn't really to get them together, see. It's because I want them both to see me *here*. So that I can say what I need to say to them here. It would be too hard in Milwaukee, too confusing. But here, I know I can do it."

"In the Melinda Zone," Paul said.

"Yes! The Melinda Zone—exactly!" Melinda exclaimed. "Oh, Paul, you're so amazing! Tell me why you understand all of this so perfectly!"

A silence. Paul looked away from her, then back at her. Finally he announced, "I've had some therapy."

Melinda was at first surprised, then not surprised. It explained his expertise, as well as his reticence. She tried to think of something positive to say. "You must have a really good therapist," she told him.

He nodded. "Yeah, pretty good. She's actually away for the summer. She's in England."

Then he grinned at her slyly; he'd just thought of something funny. "I think she's working with some guy from the Milwaukee area."

"Paul!"

"Some guy who expects his daughter to drop everything and get busy worrying about him again."

"Not funny, Paul," Melinda said, but she couldn't hold back a crooked smile.

That night, she tossed and turned on the narrow bed, moving in and out of disjointed dreams, talking to her parents, confronting them, justifying and explaining. She woke before dawn, her mind buzzing, her throat parched, her room hot and still.

She looked at the clock. It was five in the morning. She got up to get a drink of water. She heard footsteps on the stairs, peeked through her doorway, and saw her cousin down the half-lit hallway, carrying her sandals. When Sharon saw Melinda, she jumped and clutched her heart with one hand. Her clothes were rumpled, as if she'd slept in them. "You scared me to death," she whispered.

Melinda whispered back, "Are you just coming home *now*?"

Sharon shushed her frantically, then tiptoed to her bedroom. Melinda followed her and shut the door behind them. She asked, "Were you out all night?"

"It's morning, isn't it?" Sharon pulled off her jeans, put a nightshirt on, and flopped onto her bed.

"What if your mom or dad had heard you?" Melinda asked her.

"They didn't hear me," Sharon said.

"But what if they *had*?"

"They *didn't*." She sat up and looked hard at Melinda.

"Look, you know what they think about all this. You've heard them. They think that Evan is going to just disappear and everything is going to be the way it was before. I'll be back in high school and I'll be with my old friends again and everything will be back to normal and Evan will never be seen or heard from again."

"But he is leaving," Melinda insisted quietly.

Sharon's eyes filled with tears. "I know he's leaving. And I know why he's leaving. I know that people have to follow their dreams. But I also know that he'll come back for me. And when he does, I'll go with him to Chicago. Or anywhere he wants to go. My parents can believe whatever they want to believe until graduation. I'll let them believe he's gone, if they need to so much, but from now on, I'm waiting for him. He's the only one. There'll never be anyone else."

"You mean you might want to . . . marry him?"

"Oh, someday I'll marry him. But for now, I'll just wait for him."

"You mean you'll keep your relationship a secret?"

"What choice do I have? You know how they feel about him. They've never even given him a chance."

They were both silent. Melinda didn't know what to say. She wanted to say something about how hard it was to keep something you feel so deeply from your parents, how much energy it takes, how it cuts you off from other people. But while she was searching for the words, Sharon began to drift into sleep. Her head was tipped back; her cheeks were still glistening with tears, her face relaxing, her features softened with longing and exhaustion.

She's so beautiful, Melinda thought. *She's easy to love. Maybe Evan looks at her like this sometimes and really loves her.*

But she didn't believe it. It seemed to her that Sharon was wrong. She felt the tremendous burden of Sharon's wrongness. All the mistakes to come. In her own room, she picked up the photograph of herself with her father and her teenaged mother. It hit her then, that in the picture her father was the same age as Evan O'Connor. She remembered what Aunt Rita had said about her parents, the words droning in her ears mournfully as she fell asleep: *both in love, both in love, both in love.*

ELEVEN

• ❖ •

"Is something bothering you?" Aunt Rita asked Melinda at breakfast. "You've been awfully quiet the last few days."

"I'm all right."

"Things are a little out-of-kilter around here lately, aren't they? Is it making you homesick?"

Melinda shrugged. "Sharon is so upset," she said. "You know."

Aunt Rita nodded sadly. "Tell you what. Why don't you and I do a little shopping for her this morning. Maybe it would make us both feel better. Her birthday is coming right up."

"I know."

"I'd like to get her something special. It's her eighteenth, you know. But she hasn't given me any hints or suggestions."

"Me either. I wish my mom was here. She knows how to find the perfect thing and she's so much fun to shop with."

They moved slowly through the downtown shops, both of them missing someone. Aunt Rita looked through racks and racks of brightly colored clothes, but Melinda thought everything she suggested seemed too young for Sharon. In a novelty shop, Aunt Rita held up a silk-screened nightshirt that said, in sequined letters, SLEEPIN' IN.

"She won't think that's funny," Melinda said.

Then an idea occurred to Aunt Rita. "I know. A ring! A birthstone ring. I've been promising her one since she was ten."

In a jewelry shop, they found one—a delicate gold band with a pale green peridot. When they met Uncle Ted for lunch, Melinda modeled it on her own hand. The sight of the ring seemed to sadden him.

"Come on, Ted," Aunt Rita scolded gently. "We're trying to enjoy ourselves."

"Sorry," he sighed. "I just can't believe Sharon grew up so fast."

"What we need is a celebration," Aunt Rita insisted. "A party. A combination party. A send-off for Melinda and a birthday party for Sharon."

"You don't have to have a party for me," Melinda said.

Aunt Rita shrugged her shoulders. "I know I don't, but I want to. I don't know what we'd have done without you this summer. Let me give you a party, Melinda, I need to. Indulge me."

"We could invite Paul," Uncle Ted suggested. But then he grimaced. "If we invite Paul, we'll have to invite you-know-who."

"Of *course* we'll invite Evan! We can hardly have a

birthday party for Sharon and not invite Evan. We'll make it a going-away party for him, too."

Uncle Ted lifted his water glass. "I'll drink to that."

On the drive home, Melinda decided there were too many secrets in the world and she wanted to eliminate one. "There's something I need to tell you about when I'm leaving, Aunt Rita," she confided.

"I think I know what you've been worried about," Aunt Rita said. "You're afraid that your mom and dad will fight about who will come and get you, aren't you?"

Melinda hesitated.

"Why don't you just take the train home, honey? That way you won't have to choose and there won't be any hurt feelings."

"I had this other idea," Melinda said. "I've asked them both to come here. The two of them. At the same time."

"You'll never get them to agree to that," Aunt Rita said gently.

"They've already agreed. Because they don't know I invited them both."

Aunt Rita had pulled the car to a stop in her driveway. Now she pressed her head against the back of her seat, her expression confused. "Your voice sounds serious, so I know you're not joking. Oh, Melinda. What is that going to accomplish?"

"If they both come here, I can show them my room and this place and you'll be here and Paul and everything. Then I know I can make them understand that I've really *changed*."

Aunt Rita was shaking her head, frowning and disagreeing, all the while she spoke. Melinda, seeing this, finished her explanation with a wail. "You told me not to shut them out. And you told me I could have what I need here. This is what I need."

Aunt Rita's expression changed. She looked trapped. "But, honey," she finally said, "you have to understand— you're asking me to keep an enormous secret from my own sister. A secret I know she won't like. Don't you see? She would never understand, she would be very hurt and angry."

"You'd help *her*," Melinda said thickly. "Because she's your sister. It's not my fault I don't have a sister to help me."

She kept her face turned away, but now she was blotting tears clumsily with her fingertips. In a low voice, Aunt Rita said, "I tried to help her. I would have done anything for her." She looked out her window and took a deep, determined breath. "Oh, what the hell," she said. "It all makes sense, in a funny way. My niece needs me. I'll keep the secret."

She began rummaging through her purse for a Kleenex, pulling out samples of animal food, vet prescriptions, assorted leashes. "You do what you have to do, Melinda," she said. "I'll keep my mouth shut about it."

"You mean it?" Melinda asked.

Aunt Rita handed her a Kleenex, tattered but clean. "You bet."

At the dinner table, Aunt Rita told Sharon about the party. "We'll have a barbecue in the backyard with ribs and corn and tomatoes and all your favorite things. And I'll make a lemon pie for Melinda and chocolate cake for you. And we'll invite Paul and Evan and anybody else you'd like to invite."

Uncle Ted interjected, "Invite some of those girlfriends you've blown off for the summer."

Sharon half turned to glare at him.

Aunt Rita said quickly, "Or we could have a smallish, intimate party. Whatever you want. We were thinking we'd make it a celebration because Evan's leaving, too."

Sharon looked appalled. "Mo-ther!"

"Oops, I didn't mean that quite the way it sounded," Aunt Rita said anxiously. "I mean a chance to wish Evan well and good luck and everything."

Sharon looked mollified. "You *should* do something special for Evan," she said. "And I'd prefer an intimate party." She studied Melinda curiously. "You're inviting Paul?"

Melinda said evasively, "He might be busy."

"Oh, he won't be *busy,*" Sharon said knowingly. "Ask him. Talk him into coming, really, I want him to. He's never met Evan."

Melinda repeated, "He might be busy."

But all three Parkers insisted, in unison, "Just *ask* him."

She found him on his porch in the early evening, talking into a cordless phone. He seemed to be making plans for later on, but he looked glad to see her.

"Are you going somewhere?" Melinda asked.

"My friend Rick is back from Dallas. We were going to do something later. What's up?"

Melinda sat down in the beanbag chair. "My aunt and uncle have decided to throw a party. Birthday and going-away. They want you to come."

Paul looked confused. "Who wants me to come?"

"Sharon and everybody."

He sat up on the lounger, his eyes widening. "Sharon's *inviting* me?"

Melinda nodded. "She asked me to talk you into it."

His eyes widened farther.

"I was planning to tell them you'd be too busy," Melinda explained.

"*Busy?*" he echoed. "Yeah, I'm really busy! Busy sitting in my chair that night. What night did you say it was?"

"It's next Saturday, the fourteenth. The day before my parents are coming."

"And Sharon really asked you to talk me into it? Wow. *Wow!*"

Melinda realized then that Paul had completely misunderstood the invitation. A meanness came over her. Her voice grew taunting. "She's probably *dying* to make up with you."

But Paul didn't catch the sarcasm. He leaned forward in his chair and asked, "*Seriously?*"

"Oh God, Paul. Please. Try to control yourself! Evan isn't gone yet; he'll be there, too."

Paul lowered his head, realizing his mistake. Then he looked at her and defended himself unhappily. "Look, you made it sound like—"

"I did *not*! Don't you blame me. All I said was that you were *invited*."

"You told me that Sharon asked you to talk me into—"

"Because of me!" Melinda cried. She stood up angrily. "She thought you might want to come as *my* friend. Isn't that ridiculous? Isn't that a pathetic idea?"

"There was just something about the way you said it—"

"No, there was just something about the way you *heard* it. Like it would be the absolute highlight of the entire summer."

He put his head down, ashamed, unable to refute her.

"See you around, Paul," she said, storming off his porch. "Enjoy the rest of the summer."

An hour later, Aunt Rita knocked on her door and announced that Paul was on the porch, asking for her. Melinda came out and sat on the swing without looking at him, rocking back and forth sulkily. Paul sat on the lounger stiffly, jiggling one leg. "I thought you had plans," Melinda reminded him coldly.

"Yeah, well, I canceled them."

"You can stop quaking," Melinda said, pointing to his vibrating leg. "Sharon's not here."

"I'm not quaking," Paul said.

"You are too."

"I just have a lot of nervous energy tonight," Paul argued. "Because you're mad at me."

She looked away. "Why would I lower myself to be mad at you?"

Paul hesitated. "Because. Because you were talking about this going-away party for yourself and I ended up acting like a total jerk about Sharon and acting like I don't even care that you're going away. Which I do. A lot."

Melinda stopped swinging and looked at him. She nodded huffily, accepting his apology.

"Look, Melinda, you've known all along that I have this thing about Sharon."

"I *thought* you were getting over it."

"So shoot me, okay?" But he sighed, disappointed in himself. "Anyway, I'll come to that party. As your guest, if you still want me to."

"It might be kind of strange. Sharon wants you to meet Evan."

He cringed at the thought. "*Might* be strange? It'll be major anxiety attack material, definitely."

"I could still tell everybody you're busy."

But Paul said decisively, "Look, I'm coming to your party. I'm going to come and be really uncomfortable and have a totally miserable time and suffer with you. Okay? Got that? Fine, it's settled."

"Paul." Melinda giggled sadly. "I don't want you to suffer with me."

Paul said, puffing up his hollow chest, "It will build my character. It will test my mettle. It will separate the men from the boys."

They smiled at each other. Melinda took a chance and said, "It will make me wish you lived closer to Wisconsin."

Paul said, "Hey, I already wish that."

TWELVE

❖

The second week of the hottest month came into the house on a wave of humidity, trapping everyone in a net of steam. It gave Melinda's final week in St. Joseph an air of unreality, a feeling that she and everybody around her were all struggling to wake up from the same sweltering dream.

Uncle Ted had finished his summer math workshops; now he spent his days tending his garden and his evenings in the den correcting exams in front of a fan. Aunt Rita brought a terrier puppy home from the pet store, insisting the arrangement was temporary, but she was preoccupied with training it and taking it back and forth to the vet for a slight cough it had developed.

Sharon was more and more like a ghost, haunting the premises, sleeping late, working late, and spending all her free time helping Evan pack. She took the heat like a personal affront—the weather ruining her last days with Evan. Melinda often heard her arguing with him on the phone, but then, sometimes on the very same day, she would come back from being with him wearing a mysterious, blissful smile.

Everyone complained about the heat, except Paul, who claimed to enjoy it. "No wonder *you* love it," Melinda told him. "It's perfect no-goal conspiracy weather."

"Who says I still have no goals? I'm helping you, aren't I?"

He was walking with her to the post office during the hottest part of the day. Melinda felt as if she was moving underwater. Five minutes of walking and she was soaked with sweat. She was sending a postcard to each parent, telling them to please arrive around three o'clock on Sunday, the fifteenth. Both cards had a photograph of a Lake Michigan sunset on the front and both were signed *Melinda*. By the time they got to the post office, both sunsets had buckled from her sweaty grip.

"How can you be so sure they won't compare notes when they get the postcards?" Paul asked.

"Believe me, I'm sure," Melinda said.

"Which reminds me. Which lucky parent are you actually going to drive back with?"

"I've decided it wouldn't be fair to leave with either one of them. I'm going to ask them both to go back to Wisconsin without me and I'll take the train the next morning."

"Wow!" Paul exclaimed, impressed. "You are one tough bitch, no offense."

"Think about it, Paul. How could I choose one over the other? Especially when the whole point of this is that I don't want to be caught in the middle anymore?"

"Did you tell your aunt?"

Melinda nodded. "She agrees with me."

"Wow," he repeated, shaking his head. "You're so tuned in with each other about this. You're all so . . . so *involved*. It's hard for me to relate."

"Why?"

"I don't know. I mean, I could have a sex change and my parents wouldn't even *notice*."

It was such a typical Paul remark—one quip and then right away he changed the subject. "So am I supposed to bring anything to this party Saturday night? Like expensive presents?"

"Just bring your charming self."

"Should I wear anything special? Like maybe a dunce cap?"

Melinda corrected him. "You'll be the hero at this party, Paul. With my aunt and uncle, I mean."

He grinned, glad to hear that. "They think Evan's a creep, too, don't they?"

Melinda nodded. "They also think this is the end of him."

"Don't you."

"I don't know." Melinda sighed. "Sharon thinks they'll be reunited in a year."

"She's wrong," Paul insisted. "She'll be history the minute he gets to Chicago. Man, she has been wrong about so many things this summer. Him. You. Her parents. And me—she didn't know a good thing when she had it."

Melinda scowled at him and he corrected himself. "Okay, she didn't know a mediocre thing when she had it."

He was getting on her nerves. "I hope this heat wave breaks before the party," she grumbled.

"I've decided I'm going to act extremely nonchalant at the party. Like nothing could ever bother me in a million years. Like we can all be sensible adults, no problem. Totally suave."

Still grumbling, Melinda said, "Who could be suave in weather like this?"

"Just watch me," Paul insisted.

The weather did break. It rained the morning of the party and by afternoon it was cooler and breezy. Still, a certain detachment remained for Melinda. She felt like a spectator in the Parker household—the same feeling she'd had when she'd arrived. Aunt Rita was in her own little world, baking the two desserts, marinating ribs, boiling potatoes. Sharon was housecleaning, her hair in a bandanna, her face tense and distracted. Uncle Ted was working in the garden. Melinda stayed out of everybody's way; she cleaned her room and began packing. It seemed crazy to take home the outfits she had never worn. She decided to ask Sharon if she wanted any of them. But when she got close to Sharon's door, she heard the familiar stops and starts of angry questions. "You promised me!" Sharon was exclaiming. And then, "I don't give a damn what you do!" The phone crashed down.

Melinda found her sitting at her vanity mirror, wiping tears, Kleenex in crunched balls all around her. "Evan can't come to my party," she cried. "He says he has too much to do before he leaves." She broke down, covering her face. "Some birthday!"

"We'll have the party without him," Melinda said.

Sharon spoke to her tear-streaked reflection in the mirror. "All summer I've been so accepting. All summer I've told him I understand why he has to go. But he promised me, Melinda. He promised me he'd come. What am I going to tell Mom and Pops? They'll both do their I-told-you-so routine about him. I can't bear it. I don't want to see anyone, I don't want this party!"

"Sharon, it's my party, too," Melinda reminded her. "My going-home party—I'm leaving this weekend, remember? I'm already packing."

"Packing?" Sharon repeated dazedly. "Really? You're packing? God, where did the last week go? I've been so upset about everything."

"I really need to have this party, Sharon," Melinda said emphatically. "We all do."

"Melinda, look at me—I'm a wreck. How can I face anyone tonight?"

"Take a shower," Melinda suggested. "Wash your hair. Put some makeup on under your eyes. Pretend to be happy. For them. It's not so hard. You can do it."

She sat down beside Sharon at the vanity and they looked into Sharon's mirror together. Melinda's face was sad, too, but Sharon's held a kind of disbelief that someone, anyone, would want to hurt her as much as Evan was hurting her. It made Melinda feel sorry for her—she was so much more vulnerable.

Sharon put her head on Melinda's shoulder and said tearfully, "Oh, help me, Melinda. What should I wear?"

She wore the blue tube, the same dress she'd met Melinda at the station in, and put extra makeup on to hide her tear blotches. Melinda wore the yellow jumper and borrowed a necklace and a white headband.

They were sitting on the front porch together when

Evan's van pulled up. He climbed out and leaned against the side of the van, holding out his arms. Sharon ran down the steps to him and they stood together, talking softly and touching each other's faces. When Sharon came back onto the porch, Evan following, her face was completely transformed; she was radiant. They walked arm in arm into the house, leaving Melinda on the porch to wait for Paul.

Paul was twenty minutes late. Melinda watched him cross the street slowly, purposefully walking toward the Parker house. Melinda could tell by the jerky way he was walking that he was nervous. He came up and sat beside her on the swing. He said, "Totally unfazed and suave, no problem."

"No problem," Melinda agreed gently.

He looked at her, relaxing enough to smile. "You look great," he said.

When he greeted the others, at the patio table in the backyard, his voice was slightly hushed, as if he were afraid it would crack if he spoke normally. Aunt Rita and Uncle Ted treated him like a long-lost friend of the family, which Melinda knew made him all the more uncomfortable. But she also knew that the others couldn't tell how nervous he was; they didn't recognize the symptoms—the sideways glances, the jiggling of one leg, the unusually formal voice. It made Melinda feel close to him, to know him this well.

Sharon presented him warmly to Evan. "I've been meaning to introduce you two for months." Her smile was sweet, tender. The crying had given her face a kind of angelic glow. Paul and Evan looked at each other, silent for a beat before they each said hello. After Aunt

Rita and Uncle Ted left the kitchen to tend to the barbecue, there was another, longer silence. Even Sharon noticed. She said, "Don't all talk at once." Her laughter was too bright; she was still in a state of shock that Evan had come at all. Finally Evan said to Paul, "Hey, I think I remember your sister from high school. Frieda, right? Class president?"

Paul nodded, his expression wary.

"What ever became of old Frieda?" Evan wondered.

Paul replied, "Old Frieda went to old Columbia University."

"Did I ever mention that I've known Paul since we first came to this neighborhood?" Sharon interrupted, smiling at him. "We were almost like brother and sister."

Paul didn't smile at this pronouncement. He said warily, "One sister was enough for me."

"Oh, Paul," Sharon trilled. "I just mean I've known you for ages."

Melinda felt Paul reach for her hand under the table. She hid her surprise and squeezed it. "A lot can change in a summer," Paul said, his tone dry.

Aunt Rita and Uncle Ted brought the food to the table on platters from the barbecue and everyone started to eat. From time to time during the meal, Paul reached for Melinda's hand under the table, and every time this happened, it both comforted Melinda and thrilled her. Aunt Rita and Uncle Ted seemed to be having a good time; they were proud of themselves for being able to do something for Evan, whom they so desperately wanted out of their lives. Uncle Ted even proposed a toast to him: "To your upcoming success in the music business."

Melinda looked at Sharon—she was blinking to keep

her eyes from brimming over—and then at Paul, who was watching Sharon, his expression unreadable. When they gave Sharon the peridot ring, she seemed genuinely touched by it; she put it on her small, pretty hand and held it out for everyone to admire. Then she lifted her hand to the side of her face, batted her eyes, and asked, "Does it match?"

"Your complexion?" Paul asked back.

Everyone laughed. Sharon stuck out her tongue good naturedly. When the meal was finished, Paul stood up at the table and announced, "I have to get back early."

"But you have to stay for dessert, Paul!" Uncle Ted protested.

"Chocolate cake and lemon pie," Aunt Rita announced grandly.

"I'm not big on desserts," Paul said, which Melinda knew was a lie. "And I promised my dad I'd do some stuff for him around the house tonight."

Melinda stood up beside him and added, "I'll just walk Paul home. I'll be back in a minute."

"Thanks for inviting me," Paul said to the Parkers.

"You're always welcome here, Paul," Aunt Rita said. He backed away.

Sharon tugged at Evan's arm and Evan said, "Later, man."

Melinda walked with him to his porch; they sat down on the front steps. Melinda put an arm across his back. He put one around her shoulders. They sat that way a long time.

"That wasn't so bad," Paul finally said.

"You were very suave."

"Because you were there."

"Really?"

"Partly. Partly it just wasn't as big a deal as I thought it would be. I think I even saw Sharon in a different light."

Melinda held her breath. "Did you?"

"A sort of pathetic light. I actually feel kind of sorry for her."

Melinda nodded. "I know what you mean. I hope she's going to be all right when Evan leaves."

"I hope I'm going to be all right," Paul echoed softly. "When you leave."

Melinda looked at him. His expression was very serious.

"I'm coming back, though," she said.

"You'd better." He moved his head closer to hers and kissed her. Then he drew back slightly. She put her hand on his cheek and kissed him. Then they sat very still, both slightly overwhelmed.

"I have to get back to my party," Melinda said finally.

"Don't leave yet," he said softly. "Sit with me another minute."

"Another minute," Melinda said. She leaned into him and they put their arms around each other and held fast.

Melinda found Sharon alone at the picnic table, dabbing at her eyes with a party napkin. She shrugged helplessly. "He's leaving tomorrow, same as you. It feels like everything is over."

"Not everything."

"Is your mom coming to get you?"

Melinda nodded. "My dad, too. They're both coming."

Sharon looked confused. "I didn't think your parents did things like that."

"They don't," Melinda agreed. She smiled to herself and added, "It's a long story. Too long to tell you about in one night."

Sharon repeated, "It feels like everything is over. I wish you didn't live so far away."

"So do I," Melinda whispered.

Sharon covered her face with her hands. "I haven't been much of a cousin to you this summer, have I?"

"It worked out okay, Sharon," Melinda said softly. "I've been very busy."

"Busy?" Sharon asked. "Busy here? Doing what?"

Melinda smiled to herself again. "Busy doing nothing," she said. "Doing nothing perfectly."

THIRTEEN

❖

Melinda sat on her bed, staring at the clenched hands in her lap, pushing her parents' voices into the background so that she could think. Their monologues continued over her head—her mother's about how childish it was to have manipulated everyone this way, her father's about how hurt he was by this absolute disregard for his feelings.

Why did I want this? Melinda asked herself. *What was it I hoped would happen?*

She thought of Paul, tried to hear his logical voice in her ear, heard him say *the Melinda Zone.*

She interrupted her parents, holding up her hands to shush them. "Could you just listen to me for a minute?"

They stopped, glared at each other over her head, and waited. She gestured around the clean, empty room with her open arms. "This was my bed. I slept in it every night. I woke up in it every day. I lay here remembering things every afternoon. And I'm different now. I'm a different person. Do you understand? That's why I changed my name. I've changed."

"Sweetheart, are you trying to tell us you spent too much time alone this summer?" her father asked.

"I warned you you'd get bored!" her mother exclaimed. "Didn't I try to get you to come back early?"

"I wasn't bored! I liked being alone!"

"It was a difficult summer for me, too," her father said miserably.

"Whose fault is that?" her mother asked, without looking at him.

"You're both doing it!" Melinda cried. "You're doing it and I can't stand it! Just stop it, both of you!"

They were shocked. "Should I go back to England, is that what you're trying to tell me?" her father pleaded.

"Mindy, I won't listen to you if you're going to be so hysterical," her mother said, turning away.

"You're still doing it!" Melinda cried again. "And don't call me Mindy!"

Aunt Rita came to the doorway, wringing her hands. "Is there some way I can help?" she asked.

Melinda's mother said furiously, "Oh, I'd say you've done enough helping for one summer!"

"Don't talk to my aunt like that!" Melinda screamed. Her father looked away, cringing. Her mother, glancing frantically around the room for a distraction, picked up the photograph of the three of them, put it facedown on the nightstand, put her head into her hands, and burst into tears.

Melinda hadn't expected tears from her mother. "Mother, don't," she said.

"Has it been so bad?" her mother asked, weeping. "Have you been so very unhappy?"

"Oh, Liz," Aunt Rita entreated, coming forward, but Melinda's mother took a step away from her. They stared at each other. Her father took the moment to clutch Melinda's arm.

"Why have you done this?" he asked. "And why did you cut off your beautiful hair?"

Melinda ran from the room.

"The rest of it was chaos," she told Paul. "They couldn't believe I wasn't going to go home with either one of them and we all kept going in and out of my room. And neither one of them wanted to be the first to leave. And my mom was arguing with my aunt and my dad wanted to talk to my uncle about what sorts of terrible, traumatic experiences I must have had during the summer. My dad even left once—drove off in his car, but then he came back. And the whole time, neither one of my parents said one word to each other. Not one word."

They were sitting on the porch swing together. "Come on," Paul said. "Did you really think you were all going to sit down and sip lemonade and talk about this?"

"I guess part of me did. I even had this picture of us in my mind, all sitting around a table, talking and listening to each other. I thought if I could just arrange it in a certain way, it would happen. And everyone would thank me. God, what was I *thinking*? I don't think I'll ever expect it again after today."

"Were they pretty shocked that you wouldn't go back with either of them?"

"Completely. I almost couldn't go through with it. Once my mom started to cry, I got so confused. I've never seen her cry like that. That was the worst part."

"Did you cry?" Paul asked.

"Everybody cried. Even Sharon, and she didn't even really know what was going on."

"Your dad cried?" Paul asked, shocked. He looked away. "I saw my dad cry once," he said. "It was the day Frieda left for college."

"Did you cry, too?" Melinda asked.

"No, I never cry."

"I think I sort of learned how to cry this summer," Melinda told him. "Maybe I'll start giving you lessons through the mail."

"You'd better write to me."

"I will. I've got your address. You'd better write back. I need my sessions."

"Melinda, do you remember back a few weeks ago when we were talking about your parents and I asked you about having two of everything?" he asked. "You said you didn't want me to think that you were lucky?"

She nodded.

"I have to say this, Melinda, I do think that you're lucky."

"Oh, Paul. Even after today?"

"Especially after today."

"Why?"

"Because . . . I mean . . . look at what happened today. All of them crying and not wanting to leave and everything. They're so . . . *intense* about you. They're so involved. I mean think about it! They both love you too much! Things could be worse."

Melinda put her head against his shoulder and asked him, "Why haven't you ever told me anything about your own parents?"

"There isn't much to tell."

She lifted her head and looked at him. "That's what my mom and dad always say about their marriage. So I know it isn't true."

He still didn't answer, and Melinda said, a little accusingly, "You told Sharon."

"No, I didn't," he insisted. "Well, maybe I did tell her a few things about Frieda. My sister, who doesn't know I exist. It was the first time I ever admitted to anyone that I cared about it."

"Then tell me something you never told Sharon," Melinda said softly.

Paul seemed to be deciding something. He pulled her head gently back to his shoulder, as if he needed it there. His voice grew hushed. "Remember when I told you my goal for the summer was getting over your cousin? Well, I had one other goal. A more important one, according to my shrink."

He took a deep breath and announced, "Forgiving them."

"Forgiving who?"

His voice changed, became more conversational. "My shrink lets me call her Sally; she's a very informal person. She makes it so easy to tell her stuff. Stuff you wouldn't think you'd ever be able to put into words. Anyway, Sally gave me this long lecture about my parents before she left for the summer. I guess she was wondering how I'd do, not seeing her for three months and everything. Which, by the way, I think I've handled pretty well. But before she left she told me that I'd better figure out how to forgive them or else I'll be stuck forever. Like I won't be able to really grow up. But I haven't quite figured out how to do it yet. Not yet. Sorry, Sally."

"Paul, forgive your parents for what?" She felt a little uneasy; he was speaking as if she wasn't there. She took one of his hands and squeezed it, wanting to remind him she was still beside him. Wanting to help him. He had helped her; he was Paul, the first soul mate, the first kiss, the first person who had ever made her feel lucky.

He was whispering now. "For having this kid that they totally, totally, totally didn't want." He took his hand from her hair and pointed to himself with it. "For having me."

FOURTEEN

❖

Melinda had said good-bye to Uncle Ted and Sharon, and now she was in the car on her way to the train station with one good-bye left. They were both dreading it; it kept them silent all the way to the station. On the platform Aunt Rita put her arm around Melinda's shoulders and broke the silence. "Are you sorry about yesterday?" she asked.

Melinda shook her head. "I am sorry that my mom got so mad at you, though."

Aunt Rita nodded ruefully. "Yes, I'd forgotten how much Liz hates surprises," she said.

"I never thought she'd blame you."

"I don't think she really meant to blame me. She was just so hurt and upset. She lashed out at the likely person—me. Sisters do that. We'll survive."

"I didn't do any of it to hurt them."

"I know that, Melinda. And I even understand a little better why you needed to have them come together like that. After seeing them both in action. What a pair."

"I didn't expect her to cry like that."

"Well, she loves you very much, Melinda. They both do. But they did need to understand that they could lose you. People do lose each other sometimes, love or no love."

The train was coming. Melinda picked up her bags, then put them down again. "Oh, Aunt Rita," she exclaimed. "I'm so glad I came." They hugged tightly and Melinda picked up her bags again as the train braked. Over the roaring noise, Aunt Rita shouted, "I'm sorry Sharon wasn't more of a sister to you."

"It didn't matter!" Melinda shouted back. "I had you."

The train rumbled west; the sky darkened. Melinda's reflection, in the window beside her seat, grew clearer as night fell. She stared at herself between thoughts about all that had happened, fascinated by how different she looked from that other person, the person who had been eastbound so many weeks ago, coming to Michigan, confused and shaken and angry and tired of being so alone. *Some things I changed,* she thought. *Some I can't change.*

When the train pulled into the Milwaukee station, Melinda stayed in her seat, searching the crowd through the window for her father's figure. To her surprise, she saw them both, both her parents—her mother in her shiny blue trench coat, matching pumps, her hair perfectly coiffed; her father in a wrinkled raincoat, running his fingers nervously through his unruly hair.

Melinda studied them a moment, as if she was seeing them in a movie; such an unlikely couple, so completely incompatible. They weren't looking at each other, weren't talking to each other; weren't even standing particularly close to each other. But they were both there; they had both come. Their eyes scanned the descending passengers anxiously. Melinda heard Paul's voice in her ear: *They're so involved*. She could see in their faces that they knew she had changed. They were looking for Melinda and she was ready for them. She was home.